Forever Ain't Enough

SCANLIFE

HIS PEN
PUBLISHING LLC

Forever Ain't Enough

Shelia E. Bell

ISBN: 978-1-944643-15-7

Library of Congress Control Number: 2018912383

His Pen Publishing, LLC | Douglasville, Georgia

"How do you plead?"

"Guilty, your honor. Haven't you heard? Karma has no menu. You get what you deserve and they deserved everything they got...and then some."

1

"I will wait for you till the day I can forget you
or till the day you realize you cannot forget me."
Herryicm

Chynna hit the SEND text button for at least the
two hundredth time. Okay, maybe it was a little
excessive, but she was hot. Dray was supposed to be
walking down the aisle with *her* but instead she'd learned
some skank named Bethany was taking her place. The
unmitigated gall of him.

Dray had broken it off less than six months ago after
the two of them being together for seven years. Two of
those last seven years they lived together, and now this
fool was getting married—to someone other than her!

Chynna couldn't describe what or exactly how she
was feeling on the inside. Her heart felt like it was
breaking in a million and one pieces ever since her best
friend, KeeKee, told her about Dray and Bethany.

KeeKee told Chynna she learned about Dray's new
status on social media, something Chynna couldn't do
because Dray had taken liberty to delete or block her
from all of his social media accounts. What had she done
so terrible that he would treat her like this? She loved
him, had loved him since she laid eyes on his charming
face at the local utility company all those years ago.

Fresh out of college, both of them were waiting on a
customer service representative to get utilities turned on

respectively for their new apartments. Dray had recently secured a permanent position at the FedEx Forum. Chynna worked in midtown for a PR firm as a communications specialist. They began chatting while sitting next to each other. By the end of the thirty-minute conversation Dray had Chynna's phone number. The rest, well let's just say, the rest is more than history—it turned out to be life changing for both of them in more ways than one.

As Dray fell head over heels in love with Chynna he often said, "If nothing lasts forever will you be my forever?" It would make Chynna bowl over in laughter. He could be so nerdy at times. Every gift he gave her over the years, every bouquet of flowers he sent, every card he inscribed, included the quote. So what happened to tear it all apart?

The last few weeks before the break-up, Chynna thought things were perfect, at least perfect in their imperfect sort of way. That was how their relationship went—a rollercoaster in more ways than one, but it proved to work for them.

Chynna asked herself had she missed some sign. What had changed between them to cause Dray to do this? Had she been that blindly in love, that stupid, that naïve, that she had missed the warning signals or red flags? She sat at her computer desk in her bedroom and glanced at her cell phone again as she sent Dray text message number 251. "Why are you doing me like this? Puhleeze, tell me, Dray."

A minute or two after sending the message, without forewarning, her bedroom door flung open, frightening the crap out of her. In walked Dray, slamming the door behind him so hard it sounded like it was about to pop off the hinges.

"Are you crazy?! You've been blowing my phone up for the past week. What part of it's over do you not understand?"

"You have some nerve," Chynna yelled back, pushing away from her desk and standing up. Arms folded, she huffed. "You tell me through a darn text message that things are over. Then I have to hear from my best friend that you're getting married?"

"At least I told you it was over. Plus, I don't owe you an explanation about anything I do. You're not my lady anymore. I've moved on and I wish you would too."

There it went again, her heart breaking in two. "So that's what this is about? I thought we'd gotten past all our problems and worked through it. You said you forgave me. Obviously that was a lie."

"Ha? I forgave you all right, but it's hard to forget you slept with another man, Chynna. I tried to put it out of my mind, but all I can hear and see is you calling another man's name while we're making love.

"Don't act like you didn't hurt me, too. You cheated first, or did you forget that little detail?" She fought against her rising anger.

"I didn't cheat on you. Stop being so melodramatic. Okay, anyway so you caught me talking to some female online. It's not like I went and slept with her. It was nothing. Nothing but a random chick. Plus she was the one hitting me up. I told you all this, but you still went and messed off with someone else."

"Don't try to put this all on me. You seriously don't see anything wrong with what you did? Ha! The problem with that is you shouldn't have been prowling on some dating app anyway. I don't care if you say you didn't meet her in person or not. You were still trolling for one of them desperate internet tricks."

"It doesn't give you the right to sleep with another man and then get in the bed with me and call his name!"

Chynna laughed, picked up the hardback book she'd placed on the bed, and then threw it with all her strength at his head. He dodged it while Chynna broke out in raucous laughter. "I told you not to mess with me, Dray. You think you can do what you want when you want and I won't find out? Well, you should know better than that by now."

"You're as crazy as they come. And you have to wonder why I left your trifling behind." With that being said, Dray turned and stormed out of the bedroom.

Chynna jumped up, clad in a pink thigh length nightshirt. Running out of the room after him, she pounced on his back and began pounding him with both fists as hard as she could, digging her long nails into the side of his neck and face. Her legs clinched tightly around his waist as he fought her off. Finally, he was able to throw her off while pushing her to the floor.

"Ahhh, you hurt me. I'm calling the police. They're going to lock your butt up! You wait and see." She got up and ran back toward her bedroom to retrieve her phone.

"See, this is exactly what I'm talking about. I can't deal with this anymore. Call the police. Call the FBI.

Call the dang President; I don't care what you do anymore, Chynna." He stormed toward the front door.

"Dray, wait. Please, Dray, please. I'm sorry," Chynna cried, stopping in her tracks and turning around. "Please, Dray. Just stay, please let's work this out. We always work it out, baby."

Dray continued toward the door. He opened it and walked out, not saying a word and not bothering to close it behind him.

Chynna rushed behind him. Unable to restrain herself, she began another round of verbal assaults, something she was quite good at. Her tongue could be as deadly as a bullet through the heart.

Standing outside on the porch of the two-bedroom duplex they once shared, her pleas for him to forgive her turned to a plethora of cuss laced sentences and threats to destroy his life. "Give me my key. Don't you ever come back here. You hear me, Dray!"

Dray reached inside his pant pocket, removed the key chain that had two keys on it and threw it on the ground.

Her next-door neighbors, an older married couple, looked at the scene from inside their front window like they were parked at a drive-in movie theatre. All they needed was a bucket of popcorn.

Truth is, Dray felt his life had already been ruined. As he walked to his car, got inside, and sped off up the street, he thought about their tumultuously violent relationship. As much as he loved Chynna, he couldn't continue to deal with her uncontrollable temper. If he had done half the things to her that she'd done to him he would be underneath a jail. The police had been to almost every apartment and rental house where they'd lived too many times to count. They had been threatened with eviction at the last apartment they had because of their screaming matches and Chynna's physical and verbal assaults against Dray. After tonight's fighting match, they were sure to be thrown out of this place next.

Things between Chynna and Dray were good when they were good. They had fun together, enjoyed doing many of the same things. They liked many of the same foods, with both of them adopting clean eating a few years ago. But when things went bad they were all the way bad because Chynna could go from zero to a hundred real quick. She couldn't control herself when she got angry. She always had to have the last word.

When they first started dating, Dray initially thought it was kinda cute when she would get mad and throw a tantrum, but when even simple disagreements escalated into her throwing things at him, hitting him, and threatening him, he didn't think it was so cute any longer. When she got this way, Dray clung to the teachings of his father, "Son, never hit a woman. Walk away, cool off, and then come back and talk about it later." That rarely worked when it came to Chynna. The longer he stayed away, the angrier she was when he returned.

It was during their last argument, after she called him by some other dude's name, that Dray made up his mind he was done. He'd had enough. He was tired of the arguing, the verbal abuse, and the whole unhealthy aspects of his and Chynna's relationship. He came to the unfortunate realization things were never going to change with them. He didn't want to live a life with a woman who was jealous, insecure, abusive, and vengeful. He once thought he wanted to spend the rest of his life with her, but her abusive tendencies combined with the knowledge she had slept with another man gave Dray a change of heart, and it cut him deeply. So deeply, he sought and found love and comfort in the arms of Bethany—the woman he told himself he loved and wanted to spend the rest of his life with.

2

"They say the best revenge is living well.
I say it's acid in the face—who will love them now?"
Mindy Kaling

"Girl, for real tho, you need to stop doing all of the stupid, crazy stuff you do," KeeKee warned Chynna. KeeKee knew how Chynna could be. "You're a grown woman, Chynna. All the fighting and cussing you do and then your mouth is deadly, too. Wasn't losing Dray to another woman enough? I mean, you lost a good man, a man who loved and cared about you."

Chynna looked at KeeKee like she was the enemy. "Look, I'm sick of you acting like you're so perfect. It's not like you've never taken matters into your own hands. What about that time you put all four of Jason's tires on flat after you caught him with that girl. I can't think of her name. But you know who and what I'm talking about."

"Yeah, I do and her name was Shanika Holt, but that's a whole other matter. Plus, you're talking about something that happened when I was what, eighteen or nineteen, not a thirty-year old, Chynna. For goodness sakes, you kill me."

"You'll get over it, and anyway, I can't sit back and let the love of my life walk down the aisle with another woman, especially this Bethany chick, whoever she is. And you say you don't know her?"

"Nope, I don't know who she is. Only what I see on her social media page."

"Well, I'm going to find out about her. I need to see what she has that I don't."

"What she has is your man because of your foolishness. Sometimes I don't blame Dray for calling it quits."

Chynna looked like she was about to go into a spasm when KeeKee said those words. "And you call yourself my best friend? How could you say something like that? You know how depressed I've been since Dray and I broke up. I'm done. I'm outta here." Chynna grabbed her Kate Spade purse and cell phone from off KeeKee's kitchen counter, turned around, and stormed toward the front door.

"Wait, Chynna. I didn't mean it like that and you know it. Stop getting your panties all in a wad. You can dish it out but you can't take it!"

"Girl, bye. I'll talk to you later. I've got things to do." Chynna opened the door, closing it behind her as she bolted down the stairs from KeeKee's apartment. She sat in her car for a few minutes, dialed Dray's number, but it went to his voicemail. *I know he hasn't blocked me. Been calling him and texting him and he hasn't responded. We'll see about that, Mr. Draymond Hawkins. When will you learn that I'm not one to be played with?*

Chynna was raised by the foster care system after the state removed her and her little brother from the home of their drug-addicted parents. No one on either side of her parents' families wanted the responsibility of taking care of her and her brother.

9

Being tossed from one family to the next, with some of them being abusive and mean to her, and separated from her brother, no wonder she grew up to be an angry woman.

She didn't know where her brother, Cortez, was. She hadn't seen or heard from him since they were separated. She was eight and he was five the last time she laid eyes on him. For all she knew he could live, maybe even work, in her neighborhood and she doubted if she would recognize him. She hated that. Sometimes she hated the world and everybody in it. Sometimes she even hated herself.

The last foster mother she had was the one who taught her to seek revenge at all costs whenever she was wronged. Turns out she had been wronged a lot in life and she never stopped until she paid back whoever it was that mistreated her.

3

"You always fall for the most unexpected person at the
most unexpected time and sometimes for the most
unexpected reason." Unknown

Dray, along with his brothers, Raul and Jerome, and
two of Dray's closest friends who were going to be
groomsmen, met up at the tuxedo rental place to be
fitted for their attire for Dray's upcoming nuptials.

"You sure about this?" Jerome, the younger of his
brothers, asked as the sales clerk took their
measurements.

"Yep, I'm sure. I love Bethany. Why would you ask
me if I'm sure?"

"Yeah, you really ready to turn in your bachelor
card, man?" another one of the guys asked, laughing.

"Yeah, I am. Bethany is a good church girl. I believe
she's going to make a good wife. She has my back, you
know?"

"I hear you, and yeah, she seems cool, real cool. I'm
just saying I don't know if she's the girl for you," his
friend Tarik said.

"I agree with Tarik," Dray's oldest brother, Raul,
added.

"What? Y'all trippin'."

"Nah, I don't think so. I say you still got feelings for
Chynna," another of the guys stated. "You and her was
stuck together like glue. Don't get me wrong, she had

some wild ways." His friend laughed hard as did the others. "How many times has ol' girl gone off on you, bruh? I mean, truth is, she used to do some wild and crazy stuff when she got mad at you."

Dray smirked and threw his hand to the side. "Man, y'all talk like fools. Chynna is history. We been there done that. I mean, I wish things could have been different, but hey at the end of the day, it is what it is. Things didn't work out between us and so I moved on. I had to let her and all that craziness go. I couldn't do it anymore. When I hooked up with Bethany I found out she's a cool chick. She got it going on and on top of that I got her heart."

"But what about you?" Jerome asked.

"What about me?" Dray responded.

"We haven't heard you say anything about being in love with her," said Jerome.

"Okay, so I love her. How's that? And what's not to love about her? Like I said, she's cool, she's smart, she got her own, and definitely the girl is fine."

"Yeah, yeah, yeah," said Jerome. "Whateva. But the fact remains, ol' girl proposed to you, not the other way around. I mean, I'm all for women's rights and I support the Metoo movement and anything else that promotes empowering females, but I don't know if I can wrap my head around a woman proposing to me. I mean, I can't see a girl dropping on one knee, pulling out a ring, and asking me to marry her."

"Me neither," Raul chimed in, "and especially a church girl like you say Bethany is."

"That's 'cause any female in her right mind would stay away from you, man," Dray mocked and all the guys laughed, including the sales clerk. "Anyway, I wouldn't be marrying her if I didn't love her. Know what I mean?"

"Yea, whateva," said Raul. "People have married for many reasons other than love, you know."

"Well, that's not me," Dray remarked. "I'm marrying Bethany because I love her. Believe that."

The fellows continued going back and forth until they were done with their tuxedo fittings. On the way home, Dray replayed much of the conversation in his head. Was he making a mistake by accepting Bethany's marriage proposal? It felt weird, he had to admit that much, to have a woman propose instead of the other way around. After he got over the initial shock of seeing Bethany get down on one knee at his favorite fine dining restaurant, he answered, "Yes."

Bethany was different, and Dray was drawn to her because she was the total opposite of a hotheaded, quick to react Chynna. Not yet thirty years old, she already owned two temporary employment agencies. They were quite successful and she had secured several large contracts. Her latest was the one she recently signed with a major manufacturer and included an onsite location as their exclusive temp agency.

"Hi, babe, I'll meet you at the bakery around five thirty. Is that good?"

"Yeah, five thirty is good. That should give me plenty of time to finish up here at the office, stop by the hospital to see my aunt, and then head that way," Dray told her.

"How is your aunt?"

"She's getting better. She just needs to make better choices with her diet. Diabetes is no joke, you know. Going in and out of those diabetic comas, you'd think she would be ready to make a change, but she still wants to eat what she wants to eat."

"All you can do is pray for her, you know."

"Yeah, I know. Anyway, I've gotta go. I need to get busy and finish these projects if I plan to get out of here on time. Love ya," he said like he was talking to a sibling or friend and not his fiancé'.

"I love you more, Dray," she replied and they ended the call.

Bethany was the middle child of a family made up of two brothers and four sisters. She used to feel neglected and forgotten about because she believed a majority of her mother's time was spent focusing on Bethany's other siblings and not her. It used to hurt, but Bethany believed it ended up helping her in the long run because she became driven, assertive, and ambitious. She worked hard to gain the slightest bit of her parents' attention. When her mother and father divorced, she rarely if ever talked to her father except for the times they spent with him during the summer. Granted, he worked long hard hours in an iron mill in a small town in Indiana. The money was good and he did take care of them from that aspect, but Bethany often missed him.

As she grew older, she visited him as often as possible and after graduating from high school, she attended college in Indiana so she could be closer to him. It didn't matter that he had remarried and had a couple of step kids. Her father's wife, Lydia, treated Bethany like she was one of her own. She was a lovely, pleasant, and kind woman. Bethany learned a lot about God, life, and how to treat people from Lydia.

The first year of college, Bethany stayed on campus, but when summer rolled in, her stepmother and her father suggested she move in with them. It would save on finances and plus they wanted her around them as much as possible.

She accepted their offer and her remaining college years turned out to be some of the best times of her life. Upon graduation, she returned to Memphis, worked a couple of jobs but then after seeing how the temp services operated, she decided she would dabble in being an entrepreneur and open her own agency with the help of her father's finances. One agency led to two and now she was considering a third location. The money was good and she felt empowered as a young woman.

"I'm about to leave, Trish. Do you need anything before I go?" Bethany asked her admin.

"No, everything is good. Go, have a good evening. Oh, how are the wedding plans coming along?"

"Good, I'm headed now to taste wedding cakes. I can't wait. I'm so excited." Bethany's face glowed and the smile against her coffee brown skin enhanced her beauty inside and out.

"That does sound like fun."

"Yeah, it does." Bethany smiled, hurried past Trish, and dashed out the front door. Once inside her car, she pushed the button on the steering wheel and called her stepmother.

"How are you, sweetie?" Lydia asked.

"I'm good. I'm about to head to the bakery for the cake tasting."

"Oh, that's right. I forgot you said you and Dray had to go there today. Let me know what flavor of cake you decide on. We hadn't talked much lately, but I wanted to ask you if you've been harassed anymore by Dray's ex-girlfriend?"

Bethany had told her stepmother, and complained to Dray several times, about his ex calling her all times of day and night about her and Dray's relationship. Chynna had even shown up at her offsite temp agency a few weeks ago when Bethany was out of town on a mini vacation with three of her girlfriends. Her administrative assistant told Bethany Chynna had first come into the agency on the pretense of wanting to sign up for employment with Bethany's temp agency. After asking the assistant if Bethany was in the office and finding out Bethany was not, Chynna proceeded to bombard the admin with question after question about Bethany and her comings and goings. It became so uncomfortable, especially when she Chynna told the admin that she was Dray's fiancé and Bethany had ruined their relationship. Trish insisted Chynna leave or she would call the authorities. Chynna reluctantly left, but it disturbed Bethany when her assistant told her what had transpired.

When Bethany told Dray about it, he apologized and promised he would handle Chynna. He convinced Bethany she didn't have to worry about something like that ever happening again.

"No, thank God. I haven't heard anything since she showed up at my office. I hope Dray and I have seen and heard the last from that woman. She's coo-coo. I mean flat-out crazy. I don't see what Dray ever saw in her."

"What does he have to say about her?" Lydia inquired.

"Not much. He just says for me not to worry, but you know folks are evil these days. They'll do some of anything and have no regard for other's peoples' lives, not even their own."

"Yeah, unfortunately, what you say is true."

"I pray that God will change things around for the better in this city and all over this country. I wish people would realize just how much they need Him."

"Keep praying and keep the faith. He's still in control, Bethany. Everything will work out. Just be cautious and cognizant of your surroundings. Besides, Dray is probably right, there's nothing to worry about. She has to realize that the relationship is over and done between her and Dray. He's a good guy, Beth."

"Yeah, he is. I'm blessed. Meeting him that day when I was in his building for a presentation was the best day of my life. God placed me in the right place at the right time."

Bethany drove along the not too busy street in the direction of the bakery's mid-town location in the Cooper Young district.

"He sure did. God is like that and that's why I believe you're going to be safe and you're going to have a happy and blessed marriage. I mean, you've got the man back in church, too? That was an accomplishment in and of itself."

"It wasn't hard. Dray just needed to be reminded of where his blessings come from. It's not like he wasn't aware of who God is and how important He is to our lives. We all go astray from time to time, including his ex, in spite of the fact she's been tormenting him like there's no tomorrow. She hasn't bothered me lately but she continues to call, text, and threaten him but again, I know that even she is worthy of God's forgiveness."

"I love you. You are such a beautiful person, Bethany, inside and out, but I have told you this before—if she continues to harass you and Dray, you need to think about filing for some kind of protection order."

Bethany grinned. "I don't think it's that serious. She's just hurting. I think in time she's going to back off, but thanks for the advice, Lydia."

"I sure she does, but I do agree with you when you said you can never tell about people these days," Lydia told her.

"Like you and my parents always say, God is in control. He's got me and Dray surrounded by His angels of protection. I believe that."

"You are right, Bethany. Trust God to lead you in this."

"Well, I'm turning onto the street of the bakery. I'll talk to you later this evening. Love you, Lydia."

"Love you too, sweetheart. Buh-bye."

Bethany turned onto the side street and drove up the steep driveway leading to the bakery. Bethany loved this area of the city because of the artsy, open-air type of neighborhood district it was. There were plenty of places to eat, listen to music, small shops within walking distance, and the homes were large, older, and quaint. She and Dray talked briefly about buying their first home in the Cooper Young district. Bethany had no qualms about it. She would be happy anywhere as long as she was with Dray, the man of her dreams. Dray was the man God brought into her life. Yes, it was strange, even to her, that she proposed to him, but then again this was the 21st century. Women were more outspoken and assertive. She still liked to be pursued but when she fell in love with Dray, he brought out a bold side of her that surprised even her. The night she proposed she was nervous but she was never more sure about anything before in her life. Her spirit told her it was the right thing to do and when he accepted he proposal she had no more misgivings about her decision.

She looked at her phone before getting out of her car. "Bout 15 minutes before I get there. Stuck in traffic on Union," Dray's text read.

"Ok, I'm pulling up at bakery now. Will wait in car for you. See you in a bit."

As she was about to pull into a parking space, she gave pause and placed her hand against her chest as its pace picked up. The woman who she'd seen in person just once before was walking out of the bakery and to the parking lot, but there was no doubt it was her. Bethany remained inside her car and watched as none

Shelia E. Bell

other than Chynna strolled by with a white bakery box in her hand. Bethany kept her eyes glued on Chynna's movements. As she watched her, she could see why Dray had been so attracted to her. Chynna was beautiful and impeccably dressed. Anyone who wasn't aware of her evil ways would probably easily think she was a woman of high class, sophisticated, and had it going on. Maybe she was or rather maybe she had been once upon a time, but Bethany believed inside the woman's mind was a twisted side that caused her to do the foolish things Dray had told her she'd done.

Chynna had not only come to her place of business, but Dray said Chynna had flattened his tires, broken out his car windows, and sent him thousands of text messages. She followed him around town and confronted his friends, brothers, and anyone else she believed interfered in her and Dray's relationship. She breathed a short sigh of relief that she hadn't heard anything from Chynna—not until seeing her come out the bakery.

Bethany sat frozen inside her car, hoping Chynna would pass by without noticing her, but then she wondered, *What's she doing here anyway? Is this a coincidence or one of Chynna's schemes?*

While Bethany daydreamed, Chynna approached Bethany's car and tapped on her window. "Uh, missy, you have me blocked in," she said, looking up and pointing to her car which, of all cars, Bethany had stopped behind.

"Uhh, little miss Bethany. Is that you? What are you doing here?" Chynna said mockingly.

20

Bethany was both shocked and livid when she realized the woman was actually Chynna. She imagined her nostrils had spread like a bull's nostrils before charging. She was furious and scared at the same time. Had Chynna actually followed her to the bakery without her noticing? How would she know that she and Dray were supposed to be here at this time? Surely, it had to be a coincidence.

"I beg your pardon?" Bethany said, acting coyly as her brows seemed to come together. "I can ask you the same thing. What are you doing here?"

Chynna looked around, surveying her surroundings. With outstretched hands, she smiled wickedly. "Last time I heard this is a public place. I didn't know you owned a stake in it." Her smile disappeared. She folded her arms with the box of goodies extending out of her hand and stood back on her right leg. Her pink pencil skirt showcased her perfect legs and shapely hips. The white blouse remained tucked neatly inside the skirt and her brownish black hair rested against the top of her collar.

"So are you just going to sit here looking stupid or are you going to move from behind my car?"

Seething, Bethany bit her bottom lip and sped off to a parking space in front of her and closer to the bakery door. In her rearview mirror she cautiously watched Chynna back out of her parking space. Just as she was almost out of it all the way, Bethany saw Dray pulling up. She released a sigh and continued watching, slightly turning around in the car to get a better view.

Dray parked and Bethany watched as Chynna got out of her car and walked toward Dray's car. Standing on the passenger side, she leaned in. It was apparent Dray had let down the window. Unable to hear the exchange, Bethany could see Dray's expression. She could tell whatever he was saying was nothing pleasant. He pointed a finger toward Bethany. Chynna laughed, while glancing in Bethany's direction and then back at Dray.

Bethany, by this time, had let down her window. She strained to hear anything and was rewarded when Chynna yelled out a nasty expletive, displayed a finger sign, followed by placing her hand to her lips and blowing Dray a kiss before sashaying back to her car.

Dray opened the door to his car, got out, and walked toward Bethany's car while still keeping an eye on Chynna. He could never be certain of what her move might be. She was just that unpredictable.

Chynna sat in the parking spot and appeared to be on the phone.

"Come on, let's get inside. Did she say anything to you?"

"Not really, I just saw her coming out of the bakery."

"Anyway, don't mind her. Okay?" Dray placed an arm around Bethany's waist and leaned to give her a lingering kiss as he briefly looked over his shoulder at Chynna.

Chynna was furious as she watched Dray's display of affection toward another woman. How could he keep doing her this way? She waited patiently, watching them carefully as they disappeared inside.

About ten minutes after Dray and Bethany were led to the cake tasting area, in walked two police officers followed by a hysterical woman. The woman was no one other than Chynna. Her hair was splayed over her head, her blouse was half way out of her skirt, and there was what looked like blood on the front of the blouse.

"There she is," Chynna pointed in Bethany's direction. "She's the one that assaulted me."

"Stay back, ma'am. We'll go talk to her," one of the officers instructed.

"I'm telling you, I didn't lay a hand on her," Bethany cried as the police approached. "She's crazy. This woman has been harassing me and my fiancé for weeks."

"Is that why you slapped her and scratched her on the side of her face?" one of the two male officers asked, looking at Bethany like they didn't believe a word she said.

"I'm telling you, I didn't touch her...but I wish I had," she said bitingly.

Chynna continued crying. "She's lying. She pulled my hair and she scratched me. See, look at it. I already showed you but look at me. Those long nails of hers hurt like hell. She's talking about me harassing her but she's been the one harassing me and so has he," she said, eyeing Dray with anger-filled eyes. "I just left this bakery and when I came outside she was parked behind my car, blocking me in, and apparently waiting on me. She must have followed me here," Chynna cried. Her eyes were bloodshot like she'd been drinking all night and hadn't had any sleep. She kept touching her face. "Aren't you going to arrest her?"

Fifteen minutes into questioning and going back and forth the police officer said, "Ma'am, turn around and put your hands behind your back. You have the right to remain...."

"What? But, I didn't do anything. Please, don't do this." Bethany's peripheral vision locked in on people inside the bakery making videos from their phones as they led an embarrassed, frightened Bethany to the police car.

"You're going to be sorry," Dray mouthed when Chynna looked at him and gave him a snide grin followed by an air kiss.

4

"You never have to say sorry to me because I go out of my way to make sure you are." Unknown

Dray bailed Bethany out of jail and they went straight to a lawyer's office who assured Bethany he could get the case dismissed. The first thing he was going to do was see if the bakery had a camera of the parking lot. Even if they didn't, he felt confident he could prove Chynna's accusations held no merit.

"I can't tell you how humiliated I am," Bethany cried. "I've never been inside a jail cell. It was horrible, Dray."

Dray wrapped his arm across Bethany's shoulder. "I'm so sorry you had to go through this, baby."

"I'm going to file for a protective order against her. That woman is loco. I can never tell when or where she's going to show up. I won't live my life like this, Dray. You're going to have to do something about her."

"I will. I promise I will. It's just that Chynna is a troubled woman. I'm not making excuses for her, but I'm just saying, with all she's been through in her life, she has this, well, she has this unhealthy mentality about getting back at people who she feels have wronged her."

"Getting back at people? Hah, that's a funny way of putting it, Dray. I've done nothing to the woman. I don't understand why she's blaming me for you and her breaking up. It doesn't make sense. I've never understood women or men going after the other person instead of the man or woman who cheated on them." Bethany threw her hands up in disgust. "I just want to go home, climb in my bed, and pray this all goes away. This can affect my business and everything."

"Please, Bethany. Everything will turn out fine. You just wait and see."

"Yeah, whatever."

Dray took Bethany home, but she refused to let him come inside. "Thanks, I'll talk to you later," she said dryly.

"You sure you don't want me to stay with you for a while?"

"I'm sure. Bye, Dray." She got out of his car, slammed the door, and briskly rushed up to her front door.

Dray watched as she unlocked the door to her apartment and disappeared inside. "Dang, Chynna why can't you just be like any other normal female? Why do you have to act so hood?" he said aloud in the car.

A few weeks after the bakery incident, a still furious and not to be outdone Chynna, drove to Dray's job and parked her car in an inconspicuous space and scrolled social media while she waited. After an hour she was ready to say forget it. She was getting hungry and the cloudy sky opened and released a heavy stream of showers. She turned the ignition, and put the car in

Drive. Just as she was about to pull out of her parking space, she saw him. She smiled but her smile turned into a frown when a woman walked out of the office building and joined him underneath his umbrella. He placed his hand around her waist, looked down at her and even from where she was parked, she could see the huge smile form on his face seconds before he planted a kiss on Bethany's lips. Like something out of a movie, they walked in the rain, hand in hand.

Chynna mashed the gas pedal at full strength. Her beautiful, flawless, melanin skin changed to a deep dark purple and her eyes filled with blinding rage. She sped toward the couple as they crossed the street and headed for the parking lot. By the time Dray and Bethany saw the car speeding toward them, it was too late. A loud thud sent Dray flying in the air as he pushed Bethany out of harm's way.

"How you like me now, Dray? I told you not to mess with me."

As soon as the deed had been done, Chynna momentarily regretted it…. before a feeling of satisfaction took its place. She looked through her rearview mirror and saw Bethany half sitting up on the pavement, one hand up in the air, frantically screaming for help and holding her side with the other hand. Flooring the accelerator again, she sped off, up the street, and made several turns until she was on the interstate. Only then did she breathe a sigh of relief in not seeing anyone trailing her.

Hot tears blinded her but she continued to drive, blending in with the mid-day traffic that was not unusual for a Wednesday. Pushing the button on the console, she told Alexa, "Call Kee at work." The robotic voice followed her command.

"Hello, you've reached the voicemail…."

Chynna hit the End button on the console and drove in the direction of the office building where she worked. Arriving at the security gate, she flashed her ID badge at the guard who opened the gate to allow her entrance. Finding a parking space, she turned off the ignition, and gripped the steering wheel with every ounce of strength in her until her hands began to sweat. Her head rested on the steering wheel and she sobbed until someone startled her by tapping on her window.

"Chynna, are you okay?" the male voice asked.

Chynna lifted her head but looked away, swiftly wiped her eyes, and then turned to face Nathaniel, her co-worker, who was really into her. He'd been asking her to go out with him for months and each time she refused.

"Uh, hi, Nathaniel. Yea, I'm good," she answered as she looked away again, grabbed her purse, and proceeded to open the car door.

Nathaniel grabbed the door handle and opened it all the way, giving her full access to get out of the car. She looked down and wiped the remainder of her tears.

"You sure? You look like you've been crying."

"No, it's just my allergies mixed with a dry eye socket. People always think I'm crying. Tears come when I yawn, when I laugh…you name it, but this time the allergies are kicking my butt and wreaking havoc," she easily lied as she began walking toward the entrance to Building A where she and Nathaniel worked.

He walked alongside her. "Is there anything I can do?"

"No, I went to Walgreens and got some Zyrtec. I'll be fine."

"Hey, I was wondering if you'd like to go to the Delta Fair this weekend. We can go Saturday or Sunday—your pick."

They arrived at the entrance. Nathaniel pushed the door open and stood to the side, allowing Chynna access into the building. She walked through the doors, took a few steps until she cleared the entrance, went into the lobby, and then stopped and looked at Nathaniel.

Nathaniel wasn't a bad looking guy. As a matter of fact, he was rather handsome in his own way. He was about an inch taller than her with a nice physique. His manicured beard and mustache made him look distinguished, and he dressed like he was already a top executive. She could count the times he wasn't dressed in a nice suit. His voice was inviting, something she hadn't noticed before because she was too busy avoiding him like the plague, being in love with Dray and all.

Ohmygosh, Dray. God, I hope I didn't kill him. I can be charged with murder if that wench he was with can describe me or if she got my license plate number. Ughhh, but if she describes my car, then the police will probably be knocking at my door. Oh, well, you should realize buddy, you reap what you sow.

"So whaddaya say? Would you like to go with me? I want to get to know you, Chynna. I promise I won't bite."

"Do I look like the kind of girl that's afraid of a man with a big appetite?" Chynna gave him a hypnotic smile and swished off, leaving Nathaniel standing behind her in awe.

5

"In the arithmetic of love, one plus one equals everything, and two minus one equals nothing." Mignon McLaughlin

"Hey, Chynna. I'm sorry I missed your call. You sounded like something had gone down. I was in a meeting when you called. That she-devil I work for had me running behind her like a slave. Uggh, I can't stand her. She makes my blood boil. Anyway, what's up? You straight?"

"KeeKee, you should be used to her by now. Ever since they hired her you've been saying the same thing, that she's a witch."

"That's 'cause she is. She's fired at least seven people since she came here. I believe that's the reason they brought her here."

"What? To clean house and get rid of folks?"

"Exactly. I wouldn't be surprised if I'm on the short list myself. I think the only reason she hasn't given me my termination papers is because she knows I know my stuff. I was the senior administrative assistant in that department for five years so Darcie knows I know the ends and outs of that company. She'd be a fool to get rid of me now, but I'm still scouting for a position in another department. I'll even consider leaving the company altogether if I can find a stable company with as good of a salary and benefits as this one."

"I heard that."

"Anyway, enough about my job. I guess you've got your butt off your shoulders, huh?"

"You know I can't stay mad at you, Kee. You're my bestie. It's just that you can make me so mad sometimes."

"It's only 'cause I tell you the truth, which isn't always what you wanna hear. So tell me, what's up?"

"I need to talk to you about something but you need to promise you won't say a word to any one, not a single, solitary word."

"You know I wouldn't do that."

"I mean, not even to Cameron. I know he's your man and all, but what I need to talk to you about is serious. And I need to do it face-to-face. Can you come over here?"

"Yeah, I can be there around seven. I need to go home and check in with my honey first."

"Girl, please that joka isn't going anywhere, except to work and home. He loves your stanky drawers too much."

"True...true," KeeKee laughed into the phone. "I'll see you later. I already know it's got something to do with Dray. I just hope you haven't busted all the windows out of his car again or bleached all of his clothes."

"I wish it was simple as that. See you at seven."

While waiting on KeeKee to arrive, Chynna turned on the television. She rarely watched TV and never watched the news, but this evening she did both. She flipped through the channels until she came to the six o'clock news. It was the usual stuff, crime in Memphis. Somebody got shot, a carjacking, and then there it was. She listened to the reporter.

"An unidentified man was transported to Regional One with life threatening injuries after a hit and run in downtown Memphis. A woman, who was also hit, is in stable condition."

"Humph, how did she get hurt? I didn't run over *her* behind," Chynna mumbled. "Guess it was when Dray was playing Mr. Knight in Shiny Armor and pushed her out of the way. Serves him and her right." She turned off the television when the news went to another story, went into the kitchen, warmed up some leftovers from Sunday, and proceeded to sit down at the small two-seated kitchen table to eat. As she enjoyed her food, she scrolled through Google searching for a good lawyer.

Always be prepared, and never, ever let anybody see you sweat. Never miss the chance to get back at anybody who hurts you. Revenge is sweet. Remember that, she heard the voice of her foster mom say in her mind. Through the years, the words became part of her to the point Chynna took every opportunity to make her foster parents' lives a living hell as she grew older. She always disobeyed them, ran away as often as she could, and reported them for beating her more times than she could remember. She finally succeeded and the foster parents were sentenced to jail for a year for child abuse and neglect. One year was not long enough for Chynna. They deserved to be locked behind bars for a lifetime if you asked Chynna, but then again she told herself some jail time was better than nothing.

After she saved the numbers of a couple lawyers, she finished eating and went in her bedroom to take a shower when her text notifier sounded. She looked at it as she stepped out the last of her clothes.

"Hey. WYD? Busy?"

"bout to get into the shower." She smiled, knowing this more than likely would turn him on.

"is that right?"

"Yep."

"Want company?"

"Ummm. Well..."

"Well what? He texted after she didn't say anything else.

"Think I'll pass...for now. See you Saturday. Gnite, Nathaniel. I'll think about you while I'm in the shower," she teased and laid the phone down on the bed.

6

"Love is a fire. But whether it is going to warm your
hearth or burn down your house,
you can never tell." Joan Crawford

Bethany Thompson cried buckets of tears as she lay
in the hospital bed reliving the horrible accident. Police
detectives questioned her, using as much sensitivity as
possible, considering her injuries and upset state of
mind.

"Ma'am, you say it was a white car?"

"I don't know. Yes, I think so. Or it could have been
gray. I just can't be sure," Bethany answered barely
above a whisper. Her body ached, so did her left arm,
which was fractured at the elbow when Dray pushed her
out of the path of the speeding vehicle.

"Can you tell us anything else about the car, or if you
saw who you saw driving it? Was it a late model car? Do
you know if it was a two door? Four door? Compact?
Full size? Anything? Was it a woman or man driving?"

"No, I…I don't remember. It was so fast I didn't see
it until it was too late. I'm sorry."

Dray and Bethany had just gotten off work for the
afternoon and had plans to have dinner together at
church before going to mid-week Bible Study. Things
between her and Dray had escalated quickly. He was
God's answer to her prayers. She thought about the
Bible verse *"He who findeth a wife findeth a good thing and*

obtains favor from God." She wanted to be married, had prayed for a husband, and God had sent her Dray. They hit it off immediately, but Bethany was cautious. She was not the kind of woman who pursued men. She truly believed in the Bible and that God would send the right man into her life.

Initially, when she and Dray started talking, Bethany was somewhat apprehensive after spending time with Dray and listening to him explain about a long time relationship he'd recently ended. He said he and the woman had dated for seven years and lived together for two of those years. He ended it because the woman was abusive and had an explosive temper. He admitted that he was once deeply in love with the woman, had even thought they would get married one day, but instead of things getting better between them, things increasingly worsened to the point he realized she was not the woman for him after all. The woman Dray had been telling her about was none other than Chynna.

She prayed about the relationship. It was only after she felt she'd received God's blessing that Bethany began to allow herself to fall in love with Dray, something she found easy to do.

It wasn't until after Bethany and Dray got engaged that Chynna started her tirade of threatening and insulting text messages, calling Bethany, and appearing at places like she did that day at the bakery. Dray told her to ignore Chynna, that she was harmless so Bethany blocked her from calling.

As for the bakery incident that never happened, Bethany's case was still pending, but her lawyer felt it wouldn't be long before they could appear before the judge and the whole thing would be squashed.

Bethany told the detectives everything she could remember, which wasn't much of anything. For a moment, she wondered if it was Chynna who had run down Dray, but she quickly dismissed that thought. Chynna acted foolishly and like a high school kid, but Bethany didn't believe she would intentionally do something as wild and crazy as run him down.

"Ma'am, are you sure you couldn't tell if it was a male or female driving the car?"

"No, I can't. I told you; it happened so fast. That's why I can't tell you the make or model of the car either. Plus, I'm not good at identifying types of cars. I'm just grateful to God that Dray and I are alive. All I could see when I realized the car wasn't going to stop was my life and Dray's life coming to an end. I don't know if it was intentional. Maybe their brakes went out. I don't know." Bethany continued crying.

"I'm sorry, but you'll have to leave," a nurse who entered the hospital room told the detectives. "I have to give her some pain medication and check her vitals."

"I think that's all for now anyway," the older detective stated. "Thank you, Miss Thompson."

"If you remember anything else, no matter how insignificant you might think it is, please contact us. We hope you have a speedy and full recovery," the second detective said, as he placed one of his business cards on the table next to her bed.

The two black suited detectives turned and left.

"How is my fiancé?" Bethany asked the nurse.

"Don't you worry about him. He's being well taken care of. You need to rest." She gave Bethany two pills to take along with a small cup of water.

"Please, tell me. Is he okay? Is he alive?" she pleaded.

"Yes. He's alive. He's in the trauma bay. If I hear anything else or if I see any of his family members, I'll be sure to let you know and let them know you want to know how he is. Okay?"

"Okay, thank you."

"Now you try to relax. You've had a traumatic day." The kind nurse patted Bethany on the arm, finished taking her vitals, and exited the hospital room.

Bethany closed her eyes and began to pray. "God, please let Dray be okay. And God, let them find out who did this terrible, terrible thing."

The pain medicine began to quickly take effect and soon Bethany was fast asleep.

Dray lay in the Critical Care trauma bay in a medically induced coma, having sustained massive injuries and fractures including a compound fracture to the right ankle, a fractured femur, pelvis, jawbone, and right arm, collapsed lungs, and a brain injury. He was on a ventilator to help him breathe and had a chest tube inserted to help drain air, blood, and fluid from the space surrounding his lungs.

Two of his siblings arrived with his parents from Hernando, Mississippi. His other two siblings lived much farther away, one in Seattle and the other in Las

Vegas. When they heard the dreadful news, they made plans to get a flight so they could be by their little brother's side.

The first thought his mother had was to accuse Chynna. Although Dray didn't talk much about his personal life, his parents and the two siblings who lived in Mississippi, had witnessed firsthand Chynna's explosive temper. Dray always made excuses for her, blaming it on her highly dysfunctional childhood. They tried to understand and trusted Dray to handle his personal affairs. When he told them he had finally broken it off for good with Chynna, they were relieved. He'd called it quits numerous times before, but when he met Bethany and started attending church with her, Dray was a different person. He didn't seem so uptight and frustrated like he was when he was involved with Chynna.

His family met Bethany and although things progressed rather swiftly between them, they supported him and were elated, but a little shocked, when he told them Beth proposed to him. Bethany's side of the family adored him just as much as Dray's parents liked Bethany. After what was a short courtship of just a few months, Dray secretly facetimed Bethany's father and asked for her hand in marriage so that he wouldn't know it was Beth who proposed. Her family were conservative Christians and Bethany had told Dray her parents would pitch a fit if they found out she'd asked Dray for his hand in marriage. Mr. Thompson readily gave Dray his blessing.

Dray told himself he loved Bethany. It wasn't because she said she was a virgin either, but knowing she was saving herself until marriage endeared him to her just that much more. He couldn't wait to start a new life with a woman like Bethany.

He began to think that all the years he was with Chynna he possibly didn't know what true love meant. After meeting Bethany, he saw how different a relationship could be. Why couldn't it have been this way between him and Chynna?

When she invited him to attend church with her, initially he balked at the idea. It wasn't that he had anything against going to church—he was raised in the church. It was because he had gotten out of the habit of going, even praying, because that was not Chynna's cup of tea. That was one of the issues his parents and siblings had with Chynna but because Dray loved her, they accepted her, flaws and all.

Sitting inside a church for the first time in years, Dray felt a sense of calm, peace, and divine serenity. He missed the fellowship, the choir singing, the preaching, and couldn't imagine how he had pushed God aside for so long. Things were so much better now that he was with the woman he believed was the perfect woman for him—minus the drama and craziness.

He and Chynna had a mind blowing sexual relationship, and that was what Dray believed kept him going back to her. Had he somehow mistaken sex and lust for love? Not being in an intimate relationship with Bethany, at least not on a sexual level, made them closer than he could ever have imagined. He thought about what he used to tell Chynna all the time: *"If nothing lasts forever will you be my forever?"* Chynna never took him seriously and thought he was quirky whenever he told her that. He came to the conclusion that she found it quirky and silly because it wasn't meant for her. It must have been meant for a woman like Bethany. Bethany cried when he first said those words to her. She couldn't wait to become his forever bride.

7

"The best way to find out if you can trust somebody is to trust them." Ernest Hemingway

"You did what?" KeeKee screamed and paced heavily across the engineered hardwood floors. "What is wrong with you, Chynna? You've done some crazy things, but nothing like this. Oh, God, you could go to prison for years. I can't believe this," cried KeeKee.

"It's *his* fault. If he hadn't dumped me for no reason then none of this would have happened. When I saw him and that slut together I lost it! I went to see if we could talk. I had made up my mind if he told me that it was over and there was no way we would ever get back together again, I was going to just leave it alone. Go on with my life, you know? But noooo, he had to walk out of the building all kissy face with that ugly...."

"Stop it! The man might die, Chynna. Do you understand that?"

"Yeah, and if he does he deserves it," Chynna cried.

"You don't mean that. You love Dray. If he were to die because of you, you and I both know you would never forgive yourself. Be real. This is me you're taking to, Chynna. You've got to turn yourself in. That's all there is to it."

For the first time since they became best friends, KeeKee came to the stark and scary realization something was mentally unstable with Chynna. How

could she do what she'd done and not be sorry about it?
It was like she wished Dray would die.

"My God, what did they do to you that was so bad,
Chynna?"

"He hurt me, Kee. He betrayed me. Nobody and I
mean nobody gets away with messing over me."

"I'm not talking about Dray now. I'm talking about
your parents, your foster parents, the system? What did
they do to you to make you like this?"

"They didn't do anything to me but make me a
strong woman, a woman who doesn't accept crap from
anybody. I gave Dray my heart and he walked all over it.
For that he has to pay, KeeKee. Don't you see that?
Then again, I guess you can't understand where I'm
coming from. You had the perfect childhood, the perfect
parents. You attended the best schools and you were the
most popular girl in school. Everything you've ever told
me about your life growing up was what I could only
dream of. But me, I was knocked around, abused, and
molested. I was separated from my little brother. To this
day I don't know where he is, don't even know if he's
alive. My parents loved drugs more than they loved us.
Nobody gave me a thing, Kee. Don't you see? I worked
hard, put myself through college. When I lived with one
of the seven or so foster parents I was placed with I used
to have to sleep sometimes on park benches to keep from
being raped. But you know, it's okay because I survived.
As for the one who tried to rape me, I stabbed him one
night in his sleep and I don't regret it. He didn't die but I
sure wished he had. When I was placed with my last
foster mom she taught me how to defend myself, to keep

my heart intact, and I remembered that. I have her to thank for my strength, my resilience. I have her to thank for teaching me that nobody walks out of my life without paying the piper."

Tears flooded KeeKee's eyes as she listened to her best friend. Chynna was a hurt, bruised woman. How she wished she could help her.

"I'm so sorry, Chynna. I'm sorry about all the horrible things that happened to you. Believe me I really am, but you can't live your life being angry and vengeful. You need to turn yourself in. Please, Chynna. You need to get some help."

"Help? Girl, please." Chynna shooed KeeKee away with a wave of her hand. "I'm not turning myself in. If the police want me they'll have to find me."

"I don't know what to say," KeeKee cried, wiping tears from her face as soon as they fell.

"Stop all that boohooing. If I go to jail just keep some money on my books," Chynna laughed loudly.

"Stop it. None of this is funny. I'm scared for you, and I feel horrible about Dray and…and—"

"Don't you say it, Kee. You better not say you feel bad about that trick he was with. If I can't have Dray, I'm not going to let him be happy with anyone else. Anyway, he doesn't love her. He's only marrying her to get back at me."

KeeKee was scared. Chynna was irrational. Should she turn her in? But Chynna was her best friend. Even though she could be violent, even though she'd done something so terrible as this, she still cared about her and their friendship. Chynna had helped her with a lot of things over the years. She was her confidante. She could rely on her to do whatever she could to help her. She was the true definition of a best friend. But this, this was too much for her to digest. *Oh, God what do I do?*

"I was thinking Saturday we could go dress shopping," Chynna said out of the blue like absolutely nothing had happened and she was as innocent as a baby.

"Dress shopping? For what? Where are you going?"

"I want to try on wedding dresses. I've seen some really cute ones online, but I want to go to an actual bridal shop, maybe David's Bridal or there's another small boutique I found online that's in Lakeland, Tennessee. We could drive up there, have lunch, and you know do some girl stuff. Oh, and did I tell you that fool Nathaniel from work asked me out again? I guess while Dray is recuperating, it won't hurt if I go out with him. What do you think?"

KeeKee sat down in the chair in the small living space. "I think you cannot be serious about him and you definitely cannot be serious about going to try on wedding dresses." She eyed Chynna nervously.

"As a heart attack," Chynna replied, kicked back on the sofa, and turned on the television.

8

"Better to be strong than pretty and useless." Saintcrow

"Did you have a good time?" Nathaniel asked as they arrived at her apartment.

"Yeah, I did. I haven't been to the fair since...well, I've never been to the fair," she said after she thought about it.

"Seriously? You've got to be kidding."

She sat in the car and looked at him. "Why would I joke about something like that?"

"I guess. Well, I thought everyone had gone to the fair at one time or another."

"Well, you guessed wrong. Hey, why don't we go to your place? You do live alone, don't you? Or do you still live with your momma?" she joked.

"I have a roommate, but it's cool. We can still go to my place if that's what you want."

"Okay, let's go. Oh, and I hope you have something to drink. If you don't I have a bottle of Crown in my apartment; I can run inside and get it."

"Or we can just go inside your apartment and chill since we're here."

"Uh, no problem with that either. Come on," she said, jumping out of the car and darting toward her apartment with Nathaniel jogging behind like a lovesick puppy.

Once inside she went straight to the kitchen. In her navy multi-colored romper that rested just above her upper thigh, she leaned over so Nathaniel could get a good view of her back assets, opened the bottom cabinet in the galley styled kitchen, and pulled out the bottle of Crown.

Still leaning over, she said, "Look up there and get two glasses please." She stood up slowly, pointing toward the cabinet next to where he was standing, feeling the power of his gaze.

He poured them each a glass of Crown on ice before she led him into the living room, turning on her iPad along the way. Jill Scott's "Crown Royal on Ice" played in the background.

"How coincidental is that?" he said in a deep throaty tone.

"Yeah, how coincidental," she smiled as he wrapped his arm around her waist, closing the space between them.

They sat down and talked and drank. Chynna actually enjoyed Nathaniel's company. He was rather cool. If things didn't work out between her and Dray, she would definitely give him a shot, or better yet even if things did work out for her and Dray, she could keep Nathaniel as her sidepiece. Until then, she planned to enjoy the evening and her life until Dray came to his senses.

It had been a week and she hadn't heard anything else about the accident, except what she read online, and that could be unreliable. The last she read, Dray was in a coma and his slutty, wanna-be girlfriend was still listed in stable condition. That meant the wench was okay. *Dang, some things take time,* she thought before turning her thoughts from Dray to Nathaniel.

Nathaniel took the last swallow of his second drink, set it on the coffee table in front of him, and gathered her in his arms. His kisses were hot and heavy and even if she wanted to, which she didn't, she couldn't deny the desire mounting inside her. His hands caressed her thighs as they easily made their way underneath her romper. All the air expelled from his lungs as he gasped when his hands, expecting to feel her panties, instead met the softness of her womanly flesh. His kisses grew harder, sending fire through every nerve in her body. One hand swept to the back of her neck as he kissed the hollow of her throat. While he explored her mouth, she tasted him with a new hunger and unbridled desire. All he wanted to do was enjoy her totally and completely—which he did while Chynna imagined she was in Dray's arms.

9

"Persuasion is better than force." Aesop

KeeKee contemplated talking to Cameron but Chynna had confided in her and as her best friend, KeeKee didn't want to betray that trust. Chynna had experienced enough bad, heartbreaking things in her life. If she turned her back on her now, she wouldn't have anyone. Then again, she thought about the consequences she faced if she didn't go to the police about her friend and then somehow they discovered she knew about what Chynna had done—she could be in jail right alongside Chynna for harboring a fugitive. Was that a chance she was willing to take? The more she contemplated about what she should do, she realized there was no way she would turn Chynna in. She was so worried about Chynna to the point she could barely concentrate at work or at home.

"Hey, you think that loony friend of yours had something to do with that hit and run? I mean, you did say she can get a little abusive at times," Cameron asked KeeKee, but not sounding serious.

"Yeah she can be, but Chynna wouldn't dare do anything as terrible as running down Dray. She loves that man too much." Part of her believed what she told Cameron, while the other side of her brain knew that her friend was capable of the vilest of acts.

Shelia E. Bell

"They said they think it was a white or light gray late model car."

"And?" remarked KeeKee.

"Well, Chynna has a pearl white Avalon."

"So? Like I said, she wouldn't do anything like that. No telling who hit Dray. These kids in Memphis are wild and crazy. They have no regard for other people. You know that."

"Yeah, that's true. I just know how quick Chynna can flip. But you're right; I don't think she'd do something like that either. I was just kidding when I suggested that."

KeeKee exhaled lightly, glad Cameron was convinced of Chynna's innocence. If only it were true. "Come on, let's go to bed. I'm exhausted. I've had a long day. That she-devil boss of mine is about to drive me up the wall with her outlandish demands."

"Babe, how many times do I have to tell you not to let her stress you out. Do your job to the best of your ability and let the chips fall where they may," Cameron advised. "The worst thing that could happen is she could terminate you and that won't be the end of the world either."

KeeKee eyed him like he was a stranger before she thought about what he said and answered. "You're right. I can always just go out and find another job."

"You're sounding sarcastic, but I'm telling you, if that door shuts, another one will open. You're good at what you do. Why do you think you were awarded Tennessee's Administrative Professional of the Year? I'll tell you why; it's because you know your stuff. You'll have no problem getting transferred to another department if that's what you want or finding a job outside of that company. I just don't want you to be stressing, baby. Not about that job or your new boss, and definitely not about whatever Chynna has gotten herself involved in." He walked up to her, positioned himself next to her, and lightly pressed his lips to hers. Her body became alive and she forgot all about work and Chynna's dilemma.

Chynna and Nathaniel woke up early Sunday morning and picked up where they'd left off in the wee hours of the morning. There was no denying it; Nathaniel was the bomb and she liked him; like it or not Dray better watch out or she was going to be the one replacing him, not the other way around.

After their last round of lovemaking, they enjoyed one another in the shower, got dressed, and made plans to go to a restaurant for breakfast. Chynna kept her bathroom stocked with extra toiletries like toothbrushes and deodorant. She shared the items with Nathaniel. While he was brushing his teeth, Chynna's cell phone rang.

"Did you try to kill our brother?" the girl on the other end said.

"What? Are you kidding me? Who the hell is this?"

"You know darn well who this is. It's Charlotte. And you heard what I said— did you try to kill my brother and his fiancé?"

"Don't you ever in life call me talkin' this kinda bullcrap. Who do you think I am? Dray and that shaky, two-bit heffa, he calls himself in love with are not worth me letting their names come outta my mouth, let alone try to kill 'em! I'm not the one, baby. Now miss me with your bull and don't ever dial my digits again or you'll be sorry. Don't believe me, try me." Chynna ended the call abruptly.

"Whoa, you allright there, boo?"

"Yeah, I'm good."

"What was that about?"

"Nothing that's worth even talkin' bout. Let's get out of here. I'm starving." She walked up on Nathaniel, stood on her tiptoes, and kissed him.

"Watch out or we'll never get outta here to eat, pretty lady." He smacked her on the bottom, kissed her again, and they left.

Chynna was pissed Dray's sister had the nerve to dial her number. If Nathaniel hadn't been there, she would have really told Charlotte exactly where she could go and how to get there. She wasn't sorry about a darn thing, especially not plowing down Dray's sorry behind. If she could do it again, she would. At first she felt bad about what she'd done, but that feeling quickly passed. And now that Nathaniel proved that he could satisfy her needs, she couldn't care less what the future held for her and Dray. If he wanted her back, he needed to get up out of that hospital bed and come knocking on her door on bended knee and beg her to come back. Then and only then would she consider giving him a second chance.

Nathaniel didn't know who the person on the other end of the phone was, but Chynna didn't back down on telling whoever it was how she felt. He loved the fire in her. And thinking about last night....and this morning, this girl was da bomb.

They had breakfast and then went back to his place where they spent the remainder of the morning and the early afternoon together before he drove Chynna back home.

10

"The one being carried does not realize how far away the town is." Nigerian Proverb

It had been two weeks now since the hit-and-run. While MPD added the case to the pile-up of cases they already had, the importance of finding who ran down Draymond Hawkins and his fiancé seemed to grow increasingly less. Each time Dray's family or Bethany asked about the status, there was nothing new to share. It was frustrating to see how little value even the police seemed to have for a black man's life.

Doctors slowly brought Dray out of the medical coma. So far so good. His chances of survival increased with each small milestone he made. He opened his eyes slowly and looked around the hospital room to see the faces of his mother, one of his siblings, and Bethany. His mind was foggy and confused, and he had no idea where he was and why it hurt like hell when he tried to move. Again, with his eyes, he scanned his body ever so slowly, seeing his legs and his arm in blue casts. An IV was in his right hand and he saw other tubes, one leading to his nose.

"He's awake!" Bethany cried out and rushed to Dray's side, followed by his mother and his youngest sister. Bethany had been released from the hospital a few days after the accident. Though she wore a cast she was able to get around. That she was thankful for. Seeing Dray open his eyes, she was elated.

What are they doing here and why are they crying like they're at somebody's funeral? Dray thought. Had he died and they were staring at his lifeless body? He could feel himself becoming frightened. As he tried to talk, words would not come out because his throat was obstructed by something. Tears came to his eyes. *What's happening? What's wrong with me?*

"It's going to be okay," his mother said as Bethany pushed the CALL button for the nurse to come in and check on him.

Less than two minutes after pushing the call button, a nurse arrived and smiled when she walked over to Dray's bedside. "You're awake. Just take it easy," she told him. "I imagine you want to know where you are, huh?"

Dray followed her with his eyes and managed to grunt. "You're in the hospital. You were involved in a pretty bad accident. You fractured quite a few bones, but rest assured, we're taking good care of you. You have a breathing tube and chest tube, so you can't talk right now." Her voice was calming and she expressed empathy toward him.

He looked at Bethany and then his sister and mother.

"Sweetheart, you're going to be fine," Bethany cried, squeezing her fiancé's hand tenderly. She still had a hard time accepting what had happened. Though she didn't have proof, after listening to Dray's sisters, she had begun to believe that it *had* to have been Chynna who plowed down her fiancé. If it *was* Chynna who did it, the woman had to be mentally deranged— for real. She thought the shenanigans Chynna pulled at the bakery were beyond believable, but if she had actually tried to commit murder…. *God, please let the police find out who did this, and if it was Chynna, please let them get her off the streets before she succeeds in totally destroying our lives.*

Dray looked at Bethany and studied her face before shifting his eyes to his mother. He was trying hard to understand exactly what happened. His body was in pain, he felt woozy, and out of sorts. All he heard the nurse say was that he was in the hospital with some broken bones because he had an accident. Was it a car accident? Is that what she meant by accident? He felt so uncomfortable with the tube in his nose and it felt like an elephant was sitting on his chest. He wanted to ask if Chynna had been to the hospital to see him but words refused to come out.

"Are you in pain?" the nurse asked.

Dray slowly and ever so slightly nodded and batted his eyes.

The nurse obliged by administering a shot that rendered Dray unconscious in minutes.

Dray remained hospitalized for several weeks. God prevailed and by the time he was discharged, he had been taken off the ventilator, had the chest tube removed, and his broken bones were slowly healing. He was sent to the rehab facility adjacent to the hospital where he would undergo extensive physical and occupational therapy.

Bethany had the last of the furniture and other items placed inside the two-bedroom mid-town bungalow she had found and rented while Dray was still in rehab. The wedding was supposed to be in less than two months, but the way things were going, it was unlikely that it would go off as planned. Yet, Dray told her not to postpone it.

Beth was left to handle the move-in without her fiancé. Her sister and best friend promised to come by after they got off work to help her organize things like dishes, toiletries, place pictures throughout the quaint space and make it look welcoming, like a home.

The more she worked around the empty house thinking about how she and Dray were supposed to start their lives together as one, the sadder and more depressed she became. She cried often. Although she was thankful God had saved Dray's life, she was uncertain about what the future held. She loved Dray but she wasn't anticipating taking care of another human being for the rest of her life. She understood if they got married as planned they would make vows to remain by each other's sides for richer or poorer, better or worse, sickness and health, til death do them part, but this was so sudden and she felt like a curve ball had been thrown her way.

Dray wanted her to concentrate on staying at home and being a homemaker and stay-at-home mom, which was something else Bethany didn't quite agree with. She had her own businesses, was a successful entrepreneur, was young and eager to operate more businesses, and that's the way she envisioned her life. Children would have to come much later, if they came at all. She was not the kind of woman who could be a stay-at-home mom while the man brought home the 'bacon' but she hadn't exactly explained that to Dray.

Dray's plans were for them to start a family as soon as they became Mr. and Mrs. Hawkins, but that had been snuffed out when they were run down and left to die in the middle of the street.

Bethany thanked God her recovery had been quick but she still displayed a slight limp from the leg fracture she sustained. Her orthopedic doctor told her the limp would more than likely leave in time, and told her not to spend needless time worrying about it but instead be thankful she was in the land of the living.

"Hi, this is Bethany Thompson. I'm returning a phone call I received earlier today from a Miss Lisa Webb about some temp positions we talked about earlier this week," Bethany explained to the person on the other end. "Is she available?"

"Hold, please," the pleasant sounding gentleman told her. After a few minutes of listening to music playing in her ears, the woman returned to the phone. "I'm sorry, Miss Thompson, but Ms. Webb is in a meeting right now. Would you like her voicemail?"

"Yes, please, thank you."

Bethany left the woman a message, hoping and praying she would return her call with good news about the bid Bethany had placed for her company to become the exclusive temp agency for a large, new, black-owned distribution company that had opened recently in the city. Lord knows she was glad to be back to work and doing what she loved.

Dray was still receiving a salary from his job but soon it would be decreased to 60% of his salary because he would go from being on short-term disability to long-term disability in another few weeks. After that, if he didn't return to work within six months, his position would no longer be held and he could possibly be terminated. Money was not a main issue for them because of Bethany's success, but the responsibility of caring for Dray and being the head of the household was not on her 'to do' list.

All the uncertainty Bethany faced caused undue stress and strain. What a way to start life as a newlywed. Is this really what she wanted? Did she really want to become Mrs. Dray Hawkins after everything that had transpired? Bethany had many questions racing through her cluttered mind. Was God trying to tell her something?

11

"Eagles don't catch flies." Desiderius Erasmus

There was a time, before the accident, Dray lived and breathed running and jogging. When he was a kid he loved running. That love had carried throughout his life as he became part of a community track team for boys ages seven to nine. From there he went on to participate on several teams throughout grade school, middle school, and high school. One of the three scholarships he received was an athletic scholarship to run track at University of Memphis but he had opted out and chosen to attend a university out of state. He ran track throughout college and after graduating he began to actively participate in marathons. His dream was to run the Boston Marathon but as he lay in the bed at the rehab, he wondered if those dreams had been dashed.

He tried over and over without success to remember what happened. Bethany told him about the hit and run but his memory about it was shot. When he first saw Bethany after waking from the coma, he had to be reminded about their engagement and upcoming wedding. It upset Dray every time the thought of what happened to him and Bethany played in his mind and the fact his memory was shoddy.

"Dang," he said, pounding his hand against the bedrail as forcefully as he could. "Why can't I remember? God, restore my memory. Please, God." He was almost in tears when the door to his room opened and distracted him from his thoughts.

"Hi, sweetheart," Chynna said as she entered his room.

"Chynna? What are you doing here?" This worried him even more because why did he remember Chynna, remember their relationship, remember how tumultuous it had been between them, yet he could barely remember Bethany?

"I'm here to check on you. How are you feeling, Dray?"

Chynna was on her best behavior. She had no plans to stay long but she wanted to see his reaction, had to know how much he remembered, if anything, about her dastardly deed. Plus, she loved Dray and though she was good at putting on a strong front around others, she felt terrible about allowing her need to get revenge overrule her mind and cause her to do what she'd done.

The longer she stood at his bedside, the more she understood Dray didn't recall anything. "So you're telling me you have no idea who could have done this?" Chynna prodded.

"No, I...why would anyone intentionally run down me and Beth? It doesn't make sense."

"Well, it may not make sense but according to the news, that's exactly what's being reported. The two of you were walking across the street when you were run down by only God knows who," Chynna explained, while taking hold of his hand in hers.

"But who? Who would do something like this, Chynna?"

"I can't believe you don't know more. Haven't the detectives or anyone from the police department come to question you?"

"Yes, but I can't remember a thing." Dray appeared more confused and uncertain, hearing what Chynna said.

"You don't remember anything, Dray?"

"Nope, but I do remember me and you."

"Ohhhh, goody. I knew you couldn't forget us. Not ever." Chynna smiled, leaned down, and kissed Dray on the lips.

He frowned slightly. "I remember I told you to get the hell outta my life, so what are you doing here?"

Chynna feigned crying. She wiped her eyes, batted her lashes and said, "How can you be so cruel? I know we've had our share of ups and downs, but I thought you would always at least care about me a little like I care about you. Hearing that you could have died tore me to pieces. I mean, hearing on the news that you'd been run down like that, it made me sick to my stomach. But I stayed away, Dray. I prayed every single day. I wanted to be by your side so badly but I knew that it was over between us. Today I'm here only to see for myself how you're doing." She wiped more tears and spoke soft and sweet. "I know I shouldn't be here, but I hoped you would find it in your heart to move past the hurt and at least we could be cordial. I'll always love you, but I've accepted the fact it's over between us. I…I wish you and Barbara the best."

"Bethany," Dray said, feeling bad that he'd been so mean to Chynna.

"Excuse me?" Chynna said.

"Her name is Bethany," Dray told her. "And you're right. I'm sorry, Chynna. Thank you for thinking about me, for coming to see me."

"I love you, Dray. I'll always love you, and no matter what you say or even if you marry her, you can never convince me that you don't feel the same about me. I'll let you get your rest. Please get well soon." She leaned in and kissed him on the lips again, then turned and sashayed out of the room leaving Dray speechless.

"It's about that time—your last therapy session for the day," the physical therapist said as he entered Dray's private room. "You ready to do this?"

"I…I don't feel up to it."

"I can't let you give up like that, man. If you want to get out of here and get on with your life, you have to work hard. You have to push yourself."

Dray grew irritated. He didn't need anyone telling him what he needed to do, not at this point. He knew the hard work it would take to get him out of this god-awful place. He wanted out of rehab. He wanted to be normal again, run again, live his life again. He wanted his memory back.

"Look, I hear you but I can't do it. I'm hurting. We'll do it tomorrow." Dray pushed the Call button as the PT stood looking at him like he'd heard this same kind of excuse a million times before. But he didn't push Dray.

"Okay, I'll let you pass this evening, but we're working extra hard tomorrow. If you want out of here by this weekend, you're going to have to push yourself like never before. "

"Yeah, sure thing."

"How can I help you?" the nurse asked as the PT threw up his hand, nodded at Dray, and walked out of the room, closing the door behind him.

"I need something for pain," Dray said.

"Someone will be in there shortly. We're getting afternoon meds ready now."

"Yeah, thanks." Dray turned his head toward the window and stared aimlessly at the dark clouds forming outside. It was only a little after 4:30 p.m., but the clouds were ominous, scary dark, almost black. He heard a boom of thunder that seemed to make the building shake. A long, thick stream of lightning danced across the sky. It was the perfect display for how he felt.

12

"Play the hand you're dealt." Jawahareal Nehru

"There was no footage of the hit and run on Hawkins and his fiancé. Cameras weren't stationed in that area, and the calls that have come in have led to nothing," he explained, for God knows how many times, to Dray Hawkins' family.

Detective Dan was no closer to finding the culprit of the hit and run than when it first happened, and the case was considered cold. Unless someone had a change of heart and called to tell what they'd seen or confessed to the crime, then it looked like this case would join the thousands of other cold cases stored in the Cold Case files at the Memphis Police Department.

He decided to question Bethany Thompson one more time. Maybe, just maybe there was something she'd missed. And now that Hawkins was able to talk, Detective Dan and his partner planned to have a talk with him a second time, too. They didn't want to come off like they were harassing either of the victims, but either this was an accident committed by a coward or it was intentional. If it was intentional, they were looking at someone who might return to finish the job.

"I'm telling you, I don't know anything. I just remember seeing a car seconds before. I can't tell if it was speeding up or trying to deflect from hitting us. It was just too much too fast," Bethany explained to the detectives again.

"We understand, but we hope you understand, the both of you, how important any fine detail no matter how insignificant you think it is, might help to solve this case."

Both Dray and Bethany huddled together. He was on his last day of rehab and she was there to sit with him when the detectives knocked and walked into Dray's room.

"I'm sorry, but I don't have much else to say that I haven't said already. Like Bethany, it all happened so fast. She and I were engaged in conversation from what I can remember. I don't know if we were talking about our upcoming wedding, stuff at work, I don't know. All I can say is I woke up and a nurse told me I was in the hospital."

The detectives eyed one another, looking hapless and a little perturbed that the couple still didn't have any valuable information that could lead to the arrest of whoever committed this crime.

"You don't have any enemies?"

"Uh, enemies? I don't think so," Dray said. "At least none that I know of."

"What about this Chynna Moreno person?"

Dray and Bethany peered at each other.

"You were charged with assaulting her a few months ago. Is that right?" asked Detective Dan.

"Uh, the case was dismissed," Bethany said, deflecting her eyes from the detective's stare.

"You were involved with her long term before Ms. Thompson? Isn't that right?" the other detective questioned Dray.

"Yes, but what does Chynna have to do with any of this?"

"You said you didn't have any enemies, but this woman could very well be out for blood. Especially if she's a woman scorned. And we do have a long list of domestic calls sent to your residence. Looks like wherever you laid your head to rest, there were calls made to your place, and it involved you and Miss Moreno."

"That's true, and I guess you can say Chynna has a bit of a temper, but she wouldn't do anything like this."

Detective Dan looked at Bethany. "And you? Do you feel the same way?"

"I don't know. I don't know Ms. Moreno that well. I do know that accusing me of assaulting her was absurd. I never laid a finger on that woman. She didn't show up in court and before my court appearance she withdrew her complaint against me because obviously she knew what she accused me of wouldn't hold up in a court of law."

"So in light of that, you still don't believe she could have been the one to run you down?"

Bethany looked uncomfortable. She thought a time or two about Chynna but she just didn't want to believe Chynna could be *that* evil. "I can't be sure. I don't know what she would do. But I do know I haven't seen or heard from her since that happened. So if it turns out that she did do this, I want her punished to the fullest extent of the law. We could both be dead if it wasn't for the grace of God." Bethany began getting upset.

Dray reached over and held her hand. "It's okay. They're going to find out who did this, sweetheart. Whoever it is won't get away with it for much longer."

"Well, let us know if you remember anything," the detectives said before turning and leaving.

Detective Dan contacted Chynna and asked her to come to the police station for questioning. Chynna wasn't the least bit bothered about the request. Dray nor Bethany remembered anything about that day and Chynna was sticking to her alibi. She begged KeeKee to swear up and down she was with her the day and time of the accident.

KeeKee promised her bestie she would uphold her in the lie. She hoped and prayed that she would be able to stay true to her word.

Chynna hummed one of her favorite tunes by her girl, Beyoncé, while she left work and headed to the police station. She thought back to the day of the hit and run. After composing herself, she took the car through a drive through car wash, went home, cleaned it up real good before taking it to get the front grill repaired at a body shop she knew about located in the hood. There she could be assured no questions would be asked. All they wanted was to be paid. Less than a week after dropping off the car, she picked it up and it was like new with no sign of it being involved in any type of accident. She traded the car in for a black Avalon.

The police detectives grilled Chynna for three hours nonstop. Chynna didn't bend or break under their increasing pressure. Again, thanks to her foster mom, she was not the weak, timid kind. She knew the detectives were trying to pin the hit and run on her, perhaps catch her in a lie or get her confused, but she was able to maintain a level head, decipher every question they asked, and answer without bringing suspicion to herself, no matter how they worded their interrogation.

By the time the interrogation ended and they told her she was free to go, she was surprised they hadn't offered her a job. She chuckled at the thought as she proudly walked out of the station and into the moonless night.

13

"It pays to be content with your lot." Aesop

Dray was released from rehab on a bright sunny Wednesday morning. Two of his sisters had returned to Seattle and Vegas weeks ago, but his sisters from Mississippi were there to help him gather his items and take him home.

Bethany hurried around the house, finishing up last minute details. She was excited that Dray was coming home today. This would be the first time he would see their new home, except for pictures she'd taken on her cell phone. With the help of his family, she had gotten everything taken care of for him to be able to get around the house with relative ease.

She had taken off work for the remainder of the week, and had prepared a delicious lunch of quinoa and brown rice vegetable soup, meatless chicken strips, and a green salad. She wasn't as particular as he was when it came to food choices, not by a long shot, but she respected his choices. She went to one of his favorite restaurants and picked up several slices of cake for dessert. A huge "Welcome Home, Dray" sign in decorative lettering was strung on the massive porch above the front door.

Dray looked at the welcome sign as his sister pulled into the driveway. He chuckled. It felt good to be out of rehab and coming home. He was glad his sisters and Bethany had gotten him moved from his apartment and into the bungalow. His sister, MaKayla, was between jobs, and agreed to stay at the bungalow with him as much as he needed her. Bethany didn't want to officially move into the home until she was Mrs. Hawkins, so she moved in with her parents when the lease ended on her apartment. That's where she would remain until she became Mrs. Draymond Hawkins.

Bethany would go to their new house everyday and check up on Dray after she got off work, and of course be there as much as possible on the weekends, but no sleeping over unless it was in the spare bedroom. That's why she was grateful for Dray's family's support. His sisters adored him and their family bond was tighter than gorilla glue. She loved that about them.

Dray's sister, Teena, honked the horn and Bethany opened the door and raced outside. Dashing to the car, she opened the front passenger door, embraced Dray, and planted a big sloppy kiss on his thick, kissable lips and then proceeded to help him inside the house. He had a wheelchair and some other items he might need while he further recuperated. From what he was told by the doctor, it would be at least six or seven more weeks before he would be able to return to work. He had to continue outpatient physical and occupational therapy, but so far he was doing well. With crutches and Bethany's help, he made it inside the house.

Teena and MaKayla followed with the items they'd brought home from rehab for him. After standing next to him as he cautiously walked into the living room,

Bethany made sure he was steady on his feet before turning around and going back outside to help bring in the rest of Dray's things.

"Man, everything looks nice, real nice," he said looking around the circumference of the open space. He could see the kitchen and family room from where he stood. MaKayla brought the wheelchair over to him.

"Here, get in the chair so you can go on a tour of your house," she said. "Bethany did a remarkable job decorating this place for your knucklehead self," MaKayla teased.

Dray sat down in the wheelchair, propped his feet on the foot pieces, and then Bethany steered him through the two-bedroom two bath bungalow. Everything was decorated perfectly and all the rooms were full of furniture except for the bonus room-slash-office in the back of the 1,800 square feet house.

The downstairs walk out basement, which he didn't take a chance trying to get down stairs, was equipped with a full wet bar, kitchenette, and a perfect space for Dray's exercise equipment. Another room in the basement would be used as a media room. They also would have to get furniture for the media room. There was a half bath downstairs too.

After they finished the tour, Dray reached up toward Bethany. Grabbing her around her waist, he pulled her into him. Bethany leaned down and Dray kissed her deeply. "Thank you for all of this. I'm so blessed to have you. I can't wait until you become Mrs. Draymond Marcell Hawkins." He kissed her again.

"Please, stop with all the mushy stuff," Teena said, laughing as she entered the kitchen.

"I think it's our cue to leave," said MaKayla."

"Leave? I thought you were staying with me?"

"I am, but not until Bethany goes back to work, which won't be until Monday."

"But we'll be back and forth over here. And Mommy is coming by tomorrow. We just thought you two would want to spend some time alone, you know?" added Teena.

"Yeah, I do want to be alone with my soon to be wife," Dray remarked and looked up at Bethany again. This time he took her hand and kissed her on it.

"Aren't you going to stay for lunch? I made enough for you."

"You know we don't do much of that plant based eating," MaKayla said. "I'm going to stop and get me some fried chicken, mashed potatoes, and biscuits."

"And I'm not hungry right now," said Teena, "but thanks anyway for the offer. I'm going to get home and take advantage of having the day off. When the kids get home from school and the hubby gets home from work, that's all she wrote. No more relaxing. Anyway, if there's anything you need, just give me a call."

"Thanks, sis," Dray said, reaching out his hand toward her. "Give me a hug."

Teena walked over to where Dray sat in his wheelchair. She wrapped her arms around her brother and he returned the embrace. MaKayla walked up and joined in while Bethany grabbed her phone off the kitchen island and took a couple of pictures.

Chynna sat in her new car a couple houses down, waiting and watching. She had been watching as Bethany's fake behind ran up and gave Dray a hug and a kiss while his ugly sisters got his stuff out of the car. "Humph." She thought of something else her foster mom used to tell her, *Sit back and wait 'cause those who hurt you will eventually screw up themselves and if you're lucky, God will let you watch.*

14

"My silence is not a sign that I gave up; it's only the beginning of my revenge." Inee Altea

Bethany sat next to Dray on the burgundy church pew with her arm interloped through his. Their hands met and clasped together. Dray looked down at his fiancé and smiled.

"You betta learn how to tell the Lord thank ya," the preacher said to his congregation.

Bethany said, "Amen," as did many others in the congregation while Dray nodded in agreement.

"Pastor preached a powerful word, didn't he?" Bethany said after service was over and she and Dray walked to Dray's car.

"Yeah, he did. Things could have been so different for us. We both could be dead but God had other plans." Dray squeezed Bethany's hand as they walked along the parking lot.

"I'm so glad He did. And to see you walking without crutches and no need for a wheelchair, it's truly a blessing."

"I know right? So what do you say we grab some lunch before the church crowd comes in and floods all the restaurants."

"Okay, that's cool with me. I'm glad we attend the 10:30 service because that gives us time to worship and then if we want to go to a restaurant afterward, we don't have to worry about too much of a crowd or long lines."

"Whaddaya say we go to that new spot on Summer? I heard they have a full plant based menu, and Yelp reviews are good."

"Okay, let's do it."

They arrived at the car and Bethany got behind the steering wheel.

Though Dray had returned to driving and to work, there were times he was bothered with pain and stiffness in his legs. This morning, while getting ready for church, proved to be one of those days where his leg ached so Bethany drove.

They enjoyed some delicious food at the new spot along with a large glass of sweet iced tea with lemon.

"So, is everything set for our upcoming nuptials?"

"Yes. I can't wait until the day I become your wife." Bethany blushed. "I'm counting down the days. In seven days—"

"You'll be Mrs. Hawkins. And you know what I can't wait for," Dray teased, reaching across the table and squeezing Bethany's hand. Next he raised himself up and leaned over to kiss her.

"Dray," she said, bashfully, turning away and looking around the restaurant.

"What?"

"We're in public."

"And?"

"Well..."

Sometimes Bethany acted like an old-fashioned schoolmarm instead of a twenty-eight year old woman. It was bad enough that he had to wait until their wedding night before they slept together, but sometimes he became irritated when she didn't want to display public affection either. Behind closed doors she would let loose a little, allowing their kisses to become intense almost to the point of no return, but that was it. She refused to allow him to touch her intimate parts because she didn't want it to lead to anything, or so she said. He prayed that when they got married she wouldn't be a prude in the bedroom.

His mind went to Chynna as he put a forkful of food inside his mouth. That's one thing he could never complain about with him and Chynna. They never had issues when it came to the bedroom. She was always willing and ready to please and so was he. He had to admit their relationship could have been the perfect match if only she learned how to tame that fiery temper of hers. It was scary the way she got so angry to the point she wanted to hurt him or do something to hurt him before she would later calm down and beg his forgiveness. He had memories of his clothes being bleached, shredded, and torn up because he didn't answer her calls as quickly as she thought he should. There were other times when she had slashed his tires, broke out the windows of his ride, and even threatened to come on his job and tell his employer he was a woman beater—which he was not. It took stamina and lots of will power not to retaliate when she went into her explosive tantrums. But thankfully weeks had passed since he or Bethany had been bothered by Chynna's incessant texting, calling, and practically 'jumping out from behind bushes.'

But all that was in the past. Enough was enough when it came to him and Chynna. It took Bethany to make him come to that stark realization. Bethany made him see he could never be completely happy and content with Chynna. He didn't even know if he would be able to trust her if they had kids, afraid she might be abusive toward them when she got mad. That was not the kind of forever relationship he wanted. Seeing a psychiatrist or counselor was out of the question for Chynna. Dray had tried to persuade her to go talk to someone about her anger issues, but she always refused.

Now that he'd called things off he was more than glad that he had, seeing how she had been acting since their break up. Bethany could have been behind bars if she hadn't had a good lawyer.

Like Bethany, there were occasions when he wondered if it had been Chynna who ran them down. He still couldn't remember anything about that day, no matter how hard he tried. Bethany wasn't much help either. The police said they questioned Chynna but she was no longer a person of interest because she had a solid alibi—KeeKee. But knowing KeeKee like he did, Dray wouldn't doubt it if KeeKee lied for Chynna. The two ladies had a history and acted more like blood sisters than best friends. KeeKee would never betray Chynna. It always seemed like Chynna controlled their relationship too and KeeKee gave in to whatever her demands were at the time.

"Did you hear me, Dray?"

"Huh, uh, no what did you say?"

"I guess you were daydreaming again," Bethany said. "I said, isn't that Chynna over there?" She cut her eyes to the right of her.

Sure enough Chynna and some guy were laughing and talking several tables over from where Dray and Bethany were seated.

"Yeah. Are you done?" Dray suddenly asked, wiping his mouth with his napkin and calling his server to the table for the check.

"Uh, yea. I guess. Why? Are you ready to leave?

"Yeah. I don't want any drama with her and you shouldn't want any either."

"You're right. I don't. Lord knows I've had enough of her and her stalking us. Thank God we haven't seen or heard from her lately, but I still wouldn't put it past her if she followed us here."

"Yeah, which is why I'm done. Get your purse. Let's get outta here."

The server returned with the check and laid it on the table.

"Hold up." Dray picked it up, quickly scanned it, and then removed his wallet. "Wait, here you go." He pulled out two twenty dollar bills and gave it to the server. "Thanks and keep the change."

"Thank you, sir. Have a nice afternoon," the server said.

Dray stood, extended his hand toward Bethany, and helped her out of her chair. Hastily, they departed the restaurant.

Chynna watched from her table as Bethany and Dray exited the restaurant. She laughed even louder, not at what Nathaniel was saying, but at the thought that once again she had managed to make the lovebirds uncomfortable. She had no doubt Bethany had seen her and told Dray. She could sense it and it felt good. Real good. *You ain't seen nothing yet.*

15

"Accept no one's definition of your life; define yourself."
Harvey Fierstein

Dray worked hard and effortlessly, exercising, walking, and doing light jogging so he could be strong enough to walk down the aisle and stand at the altar without thinking about using his crutches for support. He was still in a lot of pain but he refused to give in to it. He wanted to be the best husband he could be and that meant he had to be back at a hundred percent by any means necessary.

He was driving, too, but he still kept his crutches in the car just in case. He hardly ever used them but he wasn't fool enough to believe he was at a hundred. He was getting close though. He was glad he had been able to return to church a week after being released from rehab. That put a smile on Bethany's face and he felt a fresh pouring of favor, mercy, and grace over the fact God had spared their lives. He felt his faith and trust in God increase to an all-time high. It was remarkable. He prayed more and began to worry less, although he did have thoughts of Chynna. She refused to give up. Although she was texting him less, she still continued to do so under the pretense she was checking to see how he was recuperating. Maybe she was, but Dray wasn't all the way convinced. He decided not to tell Bethany about it. *Some things are better left unsaid,* he told himself.

Another part of him actually welcomed the endearing text messages.

When he saw her with another man in the restaurant, he admitted to no one that it made him a little jealous. Was he the guy whose name she called when they were making love—the one who was the main reason for their final breakup? He couldn't stop thinking about it, and he couldn't stop thinking about Chynna. He was in a bad space sexually, too. Being celibate was never his thing but he had to respect Bethany's wishes. *God, I hope I'm not making a mistake marrying Beth,* he thought as he finished up some paperwork before preparing to leave the office, and get ready for his bachelor party later that night.

Dray's bachelor party was all set to take place at a hotel downtown. His best man, Steve, was going to come by the crib and scoop him up. Because they would be drinking and indulging, Dray had reserved a hotel room for the night as did several of the other guys, including Steve.

They did a little club hopping, drinking, and reminiscing before they returned to the hotel suite and continued the bachelor party.

The knock on the door was barely heard above the loud music inside the hotel suite, but expecting them to arrive at any moment, Steve and another close friend named Jones were close to the door.

Jones opened the door when he heard the loud knocking. In walked three scantily clad ladies, dressed in red, with their butt cheeks showing and their breasts about to pop out of their see through tops.

"Put some real music on," one of the ladies said. When the popular song started playing, the girls began their routine, dancing and gyrating. They sought out Dray and gave him the thrill of the night. Nonstop they danced, shook their booties and boobs in his face, and did whatever it took to make the night memorable. Mission accomplished? Yep.

Another knock. Steve opened the door and she walked in, making the previous girls look like hood chick wannabes. Chynna was more than a pretty face, she was stacked. Her body made the men do double takes.

When she walked up on Dray he was stunned. Chynna began her dance routine against Dray's weak, almost non-existent protests for her to stop.

Chynna paid him no mind and continued to seductively entice him with her perfect moves. His eyes fixated on her every swivel. She took his hands and placed one on each side of her gyrating hips. Slowly, expertly, she followed every sexy beat of the song.

When it ended she gently removed each of Dray's hands, leaned down, and kissed him without him showing reservation or inhibition about her bold act.

"Congratulations, baby." Chynna took his hand, tugged on it, and with the urging of Chynna, and his friends, Dray got out of the chair and followed her to the hotel bedroom, again with little, if any protest.

"What do you call yourself doing?" he asked as Chynna closed the bedroom door behind them and gave him access to a full view of her butt cheeks peeping through her bodysuit, before she eased him back on the bed and began kissing him.

"You know what I'm doing. Whatever you like," she said hungrily, and continued kissing and touching him all over, bringing him to a point where he knew he wouldn't be able to resist. Only God knew, and Chynna, that he didn't want to resist. He wanted Chynna. He missed her. Needed her. As much as he told himself what he was doing was wrong, he couldn't stop and didn't want to stop.

Chynna wouldn't let up. She always had a hold on him and tonight was no different.

"Let's make this last night of freedom your best night," Chynna said. "Let me show you how much I still love you and how much I'm going to miss us, Dray. How much I'm going to miss what we had," she whispered as she took control of the night.

Hours later, when they were done, Dray was spent. The alcohol, combined with their consuming lovemaking, rendered him weak. His eyelids heavy, he watched as Chynna climbed out of the bed, put on her few clothes, smiled, and like a thoroughbred stallion strolled out the door.

The week leading up to the wedding, Dray rarely saw or spent time with Bethany. He tried not to think about what happened the night of his bachelor party but it was hard not to. He missed Chynna, missed what they once shared, but there was no turning back now.

Guilt consumed him, but Steve convinced him that he was still single and whatever happened between him and Chynna that night was not really cheating. It was a man sowing the last of his wild oats.

"Man, you were closing out a chapter of your life so you can start a clean slate with Bethany," Steve told him. "Don't sweat it."

Dray agreed, but his heart said otherwise. Since the night of the bachelor party he hadn't heard a word from Chynna. No text messages, nothing. It was almost like she had disappeared off the face of the earth, and he missed her. Several times he'd picked up his phone, dialed her number, only to hang up before the call went through. *Stop it,* he told himself. *You're about to be a married man. What you and Chynna had is in the past. Let it go.* He prayed he could.

Bethany was super busy making sure everything would be perfect on her wedding day and for her bachelorette party taking place in a few hours.

Bethany and five of her girlfriends reserved a private car on the train to New Orleans for her bachelorette party. They planned, after the six-hour train ride, to go on Bourbon Street and the French Quarters. A two-bedroom hotel suite was reserved for the girls but they didn't know if they would use it. As soon as they exited the train, a limo was waiting to take them on Bourbon Street.

For the next 24 hours, Bethany was determined not to think about whether or not she would be making a mistake by marrying Dray. *This is my bachelorette party for goodness sakes! No time to be second-guessing, over thinking, stressing out, and thinking stupid thoughts. It's time to party with my girls. Celebrate. Turn up, have fun!*

Bethany and her girls walked along Bourbon Street, stopping in almost every restaurant and café, tasting food, having virgin mixed drinks, and venturing along the French Quarter, people watching, laughing, and having the best time.

Bethany began relaxing, became at peace, let loose, and enjoyed the blessing of friends and family. At the thought of becoming the future Mrs. Draymond Hawkins, she began to feel joy instead of uncertainty. What God ordained she wasn't about to let no man *or woman* put asunder.

"Let's turn up! Yayyy!" One of her friends said, laughing, dancing, and encouraging the others to join in and they did, including Bethany. It was a real life girls' trip. In two days the life Bethany lived up to this moment would change. She prayed it would be the best decision she ever made in her life.

"I cannot believe you crashed that man's bachelor party," Kee remarked, shook her head, looked in her side mirror and switched to the left lane of the highway. "You really want to mess up that man's wedding, don't you?"

Chynna laughed. "You are so funny, Kee."

"It's not me who's funny. You are one of a kind."

"Forget about me for now. You got an invitation to the wedding so are you going?"

"I wouldn't miss it for the world. I have to see this wedding for myself 'cause I know you're going to want me to tell you every detail."

"Good, pick me up Saturday at two."

"Huh? Me? Pick you up? What? I know you aren't going. You weren't even invited."

"Uh, I don't need an invitation. I don't think anyone is going to try to stop me from coming into the church unless they want to cause a scene."

KeeKee stared at her friend briefly before focusing back on the road. "Girl, please tell me you're not serious about going to that man's wedding?"

"Uh, yeah, I'm serious. Now will you pick me up?"

Kee shrugged. "Uh, okay."

"Cool. Now let's go get something to eat. I have a taste for some good ol' fried rice and sweet iced tea."

16

"Karma never loses an address." Unknown

Dray stood at the front of the church with his groomsmen and best man, looking with teary eyes at his beautiful bride. His white tuxedo with blush pink vest and bow tie made him look like a replica of Tyson Beckford.

This was a moment he had waited for. Grateful to God that he was able to walk on his own to welcome Bethany as his wife. He pushed thoughts of Chynna out of his mind as the traditional "Here Comes the Bride" began in the background. Dray stared ahead, waiting on the doors of the church to open and welcome in his bride to be.

Bethany's slender frame looked absolutely radiant as she glided up the aisle of the beautifully decorated church in a fitted, blush pink sequin, strapless wedding gown. Opting not to wear traditional white, she was her own person, something that endeared Dray to her. One minute she acted prudish and the next she exemplified a style and mind of her own.

As she arrived at the altar and her father relinquished her hand to his soon to be son-in-law, disruption came from the back of the church.

As the crowd of guests oohed and aahed, another veiled bride walked up the aisle solo. A ravishing smile was on her face as she made her grand entrance. In her hands, she held a bouquet of white roses that matched her stunning pure white wedding gown, the total opposite of Bethany's dress. The touching song, "A Thousand Years" by Christina Perri wafted through the speakers of the church. *I have died everyday waiting for you...darling, don't be afraid I have loved you...*

Bethany's bouquet dropped from her trembling hands as she staggered like a drunken woman. Her eyes immediately released tears and her knees buckled. Fortunately, one of the groomsmen grabbed her by the waist before she hit the floor. Everything was as if it was in slow motion. Her head felt like it was spinning. Was this a dream that she had to be awakened from? Surely, it must be. Who was this woman; this stranger dressed like a princess, stealing her time, her day, her moment? Had she somehow entered the wrong church?

Bethany thought she heard murmurs and then loud sounds coming from somewhere. She couldn't tell. Her mind was doing so many things on its own.

Dray helped Bethany to the front pew and she sat down on her own accord. Releasing her hand, he stood in the middle of the aisle.

"What is this?" his voice boomed. No one said a thing.

The mystery woman continued walking up the aisle toward Dray. When she arrived next to him, she looked at him and then lifted her veil. Gasps filled the church but none louder than the one from Bethany.

"My God, what are you doing?" Dray yelped as he looked on the face of Chynna.

"You know that song, don't you, Dray? It's our song. *I have loved you for a thousand years...* Her voice was that of an angel as she song the words eloquently and perfectly.

Dray shook his head. "This can't be happening." He looked over his shoulder at a distraught looking Bethany. He turned and went toward Bethany but she got up and ran toward a door leading to the back of the church.

Her father stopped her before she made it to the door and the preacher flanked her as if keeping her from harm's way.

"Enough, Chynna. Get out of here," Dray yelled.

KeeKee rushed up and positioned herself next to Chynna, sorry beyond measure that she had come along with Chynna to entertain such foolishness. What could she have been thinking to agree to do something so absurd and so, well so crazy? This could land her and Chynna behind bars. Did that make her crazy too? Her bestie was deranged, for real. KeeKee put her arms around her but Chynna brushed her away.

"Dray, I promise to love and to cherish you," Chynna began saying. "I will never leave you or forsake our love. You used to tell me if nothing lasts forever will you be my forever. I used to laugh it off until I came to understand that no one has ever loved me like you, Dray. From this moment forward I will be your forever and even then forever ain't enough, and it will never be enough for the love we have for each other, my darling."

"You told her the same thing you told me?" Bethany stopped, turned around, and cried out after hearing

Chynna repeat the love quote she thought was for her ears and heart only. How wrong she had been about Dray.

"Please, get me out of here," Bethany screamed, pleading and looking into her father and then her pastor's eyes. Her mother and sisters ran up to her while her brothers gave Dray the evil eye. Her mother held her daughter as they respected her wishes and began to lead her out of the sanctuary, but again Bethany stopped. Unable to move, she listened to the exchange between Dray and Chynna.

"What will it take for you to realize it's over between us, Chynna? Why do you keep doing this? You need help."

"I don't need help. I need you, Dray. I love you, Draymond Hawkins and I know you love me. You always will. Why do you think you made love to me the night of your bachelor party? There is no denying what we have. Bethany will never understand you the way I do. She can never love you and go the lengths I have gone just to show you how much I love you."

"Oh, my God. You slept with her? How could you?" Bethany broke loose from her mother and father, and like a pit bull, raced toward Dray and Chynna.

Dray's back was turned away from Bethany but Chynna saw her and began laughing.

When she reached the blushing woman, KeeKee yelled, "Watch out, Chynna," and tugged at Chynna's arm, but Chynna shoved her away

Bethany grabbed Chynna by her veil along with a handful of her weave, and pulled and tugged at the woman. She began pounding her face and chest with her fists. Dray and his groomsmen tried to separate the two women as Chynna kicked and yanked Bethany, tearing shreds into her wedding gown, and exposing her breasts. They tussled and fought until they landed on the floor of the sanctuary with Bethany on top of Chynna pounding her until blood splattered all over their wedding gowns. She yanked clumps of hair and weave and tore Chynna's gown too. It was a horrific and unforgettable scene as guests scattered, some running out of the church and others videotaping the whole ungodly scene.

Someone evidently called the cops because two police officers rushed in, yelling for the women to stop their fighting, but to no avail. They broke through the crowd and managed to pull the women apart.

"You crazy, low down, evil witch," screamed Bethany. "You're sick as they come," she continued screaming. "And you, you let this happen," she turned and screamed at Dray. "How could you do me this way? I told you she was crazy. This is all your fault. I tried to make you understand," she continued crying while Dray dropped his head in shame.

The police led both of the women out of the church and put each of them inside individual patrol cars.

Once at Jail East, the women were ushered into a big room with phones on the walls. There were a few cells where they searched and fingerprinted the women. Placing a wristband on them, they then ran their names in the NCIC to see if either of them had any other warrants. Bethany and Chynna waited for hours to talk to someone in pre-release and hoping for an automatic cash bond.

Bethany, still hysterical and out of sorts, called her father. At this point in time, Dray was the last person on her mind. Dealing with him had caused enough problems. So far, they had a disturbing of the peace charge with a $100 cash bond.

The cash bond was the easy part. That could be easily taken care of, but the damage caused at what was supposed to be the happiest day of her life, well that was a horse of a different color. She didn't know if what happened today could be salvaged. Maybe this was the sign from God that Dray was not the man for her after all.

Chynna looked at Bethany and smirked. She was glad the wedding didn't happen. God had a way of working things out and for that she was more than glad. She watched as Bethany boohooed and cried into the phone, pleading for someone to hurry up and come get her out of this godforsaken jail. Chynna put a hand over her mouth to stifle her laughter. What a weak female. How could Dray call himself in love? Dray loved strong women, women who were in control, women who could act sophisticated and like a "B" at the same time. From what she'd seen, Bethany didn't fit the bill at all.

Bethany sat on the hard steel chair and waited. She was cold, tired, and heartbroken. She didn't notice Chynna when she walked up on her. She opened her eyes and that's when she saw her legs. She looked up and met Chynna's cold stare followed by an evil grin.

"Get away from me," Bethany demanded. "Somebody get her away from me." The two other ladies in the holding cell looked at Bethany like she had lost her mind. No one was going to come to her defense. This was jail, not the white house.

"You didn't think I would actually let you walk down the aisle and marry my man, did you?"

"I said get away from me," Bethany said again, looking away from Chynna with red eyes.

"You're not right for Dray. You're too weak. You can't handle your business like I can. I wish I had killed you that day. You don't know how bad I wanted to see your guts spilled all over that concrete pavement, but noooo, Mr. Hero had to run to your rescue, push you outta the way. That was your lucky day. But I'm here to tell you as long as you're living and breathing, baby, you will never ever become Mrs. Draymond Hawkins. Believe that."

Bethany looked and listened to every word Chynna said. Chynna all but admitted that she was the one responsible for the hit and run. She tried to kill her? She so much as said it.

"When will you accept the fact that Dray doesn't want you, Chynna? If it's not me, it's still never going to be you. He doesn't want *you.* He can't stand *you.* He wishes you were dead. Maybe you should have killed me that day, but you didn't. God has other plans and you're going to pay for what you've done. For all the things you've done. You wait and see."

Chynna hit a fist against the concrete wall above Bethany's head, causing Bethany to almost jump out of her skin.

"Look at you. You're so pathetic. If I ever see you with Dray again, next time you won't be so lucky."

Bethany stood, walked away from Chynna as her name was called and the holding cell door opened. Looking back over her shoulder, she rolled her eyes.

Chynna laughed and threw a finger sign at Bethany. It was almost two hours later, after Bethany left the holding cell, when Chynna's name was called. KeeKee paid her cash bond and she was released.

17

"Forgiveness is the best form of love. It takes a strong person to say 'sorry,' and an even stronger person to forgive." SayingImages.com

Bethany couldn't wait to tell the police Chynna confessed to the hit and run. After hearing this they brought in Chynna and questioned her again.

Chynna was so angry when the police interrogated her again that she confessed to the crime. She was charged with leaving the scene of an accident, aggravated assault with a deadly weapon, and assault against Bethany for the shenanigans at the wedding.

In the end, though unpleasant, Bethany and Dray attended Chynna's hearing.

In court, Chynna stood before the judge. "Chynna Latrice Moreno, how do you plead?"

"Guilty as charged, your honor. Haven't you heard? Karma has no menu. You get what you deserve and they deserved everything they got…and then some."

Chynna was sentenced to serve two years in jail and was to undergo mandatory psychotherapy treatments while incarcerated.

"I hope we can move forward with our lives now that all the drama is over," Dray told Bethany after they left court. Since the day of what was supposed to be their wedding, Bethany had refused to talk to Dray. How could she dream of having a happily ever after with a man who couldn't protect her, who wouldn't stand up for her against the likes of a woman like Chynna? A man who cheated on her. She felt angry, hurt, and betrayed.

"I told you, Dray. It's over. I can forgive you but I will never forget this." She walked hastily toward her car.

"Bethany, I love you. Doesn't that count for something? Maybe I could have done more, should have done more, but you and I didn't know how deranged Chynna actually was. I mean, to think she tried to kill you and me, is beyond my comprehension. But, baby, I'm sorry. You are the woman God sent me. I know this. I know it more than ever."

"Yeah, but what God are you talking to?"

"What do you mean?" Dray asked, looking confused.

"I said, what God are you talking to 'cause my God told me to keep walking and don't look back. See you, Dray."

"I'm not going to give up, Bethany. I love you," Dray pleaded as she kept walking. "I'm going to win you back. You just wait and see."

Chynna lay on the bunk of her jail cell drawing red roses along the border of her notebook paper. She loved writing long love letters to Dray. She fantasized about their wedding day. It wouldn't be too much longer before she was released from jail. When she walked through the doors leading to her freedom, she would run into Dray's arms. He would swirl her around in the air, kiss her with all of his pinned up passion, and they would make love for days on end. Oh what a day, what a happy day that would be.

Chynna finished the letter, folded it, and stuck it between the sheets of paper she had in her cell. She lay on the hard mattress and smiled at the thought of something her foster mom once told her. *Never go to bed angry. Stay awake and plot your revenge.* She fought against sleep as she toyed over her life and how deeply the words her foster mom spoke helped mold her into the woman she was. But was that a good thing? For the first time in her life, Chynna had a difficult time answering that self-reflecting question.

All she wanted was to love and be loved. Dray was the first man, the only man, who loved her and she couldn't imagine losing him to any woman. Before she gave way to sleep, she looked at the ceiling as if she could see straight through it and into the sky. Her smile deepened. "Dray, even if it takes forever; with our type of love, forever ain't enough."

18

"And in the middle of my chaos---there was you."
Unknown

Chynna was in jail but Dray felt like he was in his own mental prison too. He had to reevaluate his life, his desires, and his wants. He did everything he could, hoping against all hope that Bethany would forgive him and marry him, but it was not to be. He learned that actions speak louder than words. That the spirit is strong but the flesh is weak. Only the twists and turns of life brought Dray to this understanding.

The more he thought and prayed about it, the more he came to understand that he was not the man for Bethany and she was not the woman for him. Yes, he cared deeply for her and about her, but their spirits did not, and simply could not, fully connect. Something everlasting did come of their relationship; she led him back to having a deeper and closer relationship with Christ. Could this be the reason they were brought together?

Dray found a small church, joined that church, and became an active member. He was installed as a deacon a few months after joining. His life was different. He wanted to get himself right so he could be the right man for the woman God had planned for his life. He prayed for Chynna and Bethany daily. He acknowledged his own shortcomings and weaknesses as a man.

Chynna, after remaining adamant for some time that she did not need psychological help, relented and began seeing a jailhouse psychiatrist. It turned out to be one of the best decisions she'd made in her life. Through counseling, layers of her painful and horrible past were peeled away and Chynna began to understand why she remained so vengeful and angry. Her childhood was one of turmoil and trauma. No wonder she was the way she was, but yet, the therapist reminded her of how she had persevered. She completed high school, sent herself to college, had a pretty decent job before she got locked up, and so she had a lot to be thankful for. When Chynna began to reflect over her life in that manner, she began to soften. Slowly, her anger melted and she began feeling remorseful about all the things she'd done to others, especially to those who had done no wrong to her.

The therapist encouraged her to write letters to the people she had mistreated or sought revenge on whether she knew how to contact them or not. Chynna followed the therapist's advice. With each letter she wrote, she felt the weight of her past being slowly lifted from her spirit. She wrote to KeeKee who had since moved to another state to accept a promotion with her company. She asked KeeKee to try to find it in her heart to forgive her for involving her in her messed up life. She wrote a letter to a couple people on her job, a girl in school who she'd bullied relentlessly, and her final letters were to Bethany and to Dray.

Shelia E. Bell

Surprisingly, Chynna received a reply from Bethany, who was getting married in a few days, and also from Dray who surprised her by asking if she would put him on her visiting list.

The letter she received from Bethany brought her to tears. There used to be a time when it was difficult, if not impossible, for her to cry but the change within was beginning to manifest outwardly and she felt emotions that she'd held at bay for so long.

"Thank you for such a wonderful letter," Bethany wrote. *"Of course, I forgive you. I wouldn't be a Christian if I couldn't forgive others. Anyway, if things hadn't worked out the way they did, I would probably be in a marriage that was not ordained by God. But instead, in a few days I'm going to marry my King, my Prince Charming, the man I know for sure in my heart is the one for me. In a small way, I have you and what you did on my wedding day to thank for that. (lol) Yeah, it's crazy how it all turned out, but I'm grateful that God remained in control. I wish you the very best, Chynna. I really really do. I pray that you are healed mentally and spiritually. From your letter, it seems you are well on your way to living a full and happy life. May God bless you and may His favor reign and rule over your life, Chynna. In God's Love, Bethany"*

Dray soon agreed with Bethany that the way things had turned out between the two of them was for the best all along. He was practicing how to be content and walk in the path God set before him. He vowed to become a God-directed man and not a self-directed man. When he received the letter a few months ago from Chynna, he was elated at the words she spoke, as he had thought of her every single day since she was locked up.

Chynna always had that special something that pricked at Dray's heart. In spite of her evil ways she could be sweet as pie. After all, she wasn't totally responsible for the way she was. He thought about how her young life must have been. To be mistreated and abused physically, sexually, and mentally over and over was something he could not identify with...well, not until he met Chynna. But overall, he tried to put himself in her shoes. He came to the conclusion that he would have been just like Chynna, maybe even worse, if he had endured what she endured and experienced in her childhood.

He looked at his phone and smiled with anticipation. It was time for him to leave. He didn't want to be late. He locked the door to his townhome as he made his way outside to his car. He had no regrets about anything, except how things went down on what was supposed to be his wedding day. He and Bethany had an amicable relationship. When she told him she was getting married, he was genuinely happy for her.

Dray looked back at his townhome as he pulled out of the garage and onto the street. With a smile on his face, he drove off.

This was the day and he couldn't wait. An hour and a half later, he turned onto the private drive, parked his car as close as he could to the entrance, and resigned himself to wait. After almost forty-five minutes, a huge smile formed on his face when he saw the figure exiting the building. He opened the car door, jumped out and ran toward her. There she was, the woman of his dreams, the woman he always knew he wanted to spend his life with—Chynna. They had a long road ahead of them, but together, and with God's help, they would heal. Dray believed that. As Chynna cried in his arms she heard his words, "I'll love you forever, my love, but even then... forever ain't enough."

Words from the Author

"Fire in the heart sends smoke into the head." German Proverb

It's been said often, "Love is a many splendored thing." I can attest to this. But does love include abusing or betraying the one you love? Is that truly a form of love? I don't think so.

Dray and Chynna's tumultuous relationship, unfortunately, was riddled with sporadic acts of physical and verbal abuse, mostly coming from Chynna's end. Yet, Dray still loved her. Though he sought love and acceptance in the arms of another, his heart seems to have remained with Chynna.

The way Chynna grew up affected her life as an adult. She was taught to seek payback at all costs. Teaching and instilling such evilness into the mindset of another, especially a child, is another form of abuse. Maybe this couple can make it and learn how to love without hurting each other. As we know, nothing is impossible with God.

My parting words to whoever is reading this story is to look within and ask God to clean up, fix up, and perfect anything that is flawed in your life. Love can be a many splendored thing but only if your heart is pure.

About *Shorts by Shelia* Books

"Shorts by Shelia" books are shorter stories I've written to be read and enjoyed during your lunch break, while you're at a doctor's appointment, or when you just want a good, quick, and entertaining read.

If you enjoyed this "Shorts by Shelia" story, "Forever Ain't Enough" please tell your friends, your book clubs, your family, your co-workers, your social media contacts about me and my books! Oh, Yes, and PLEASE leave a positive review on your favorite online literary site!

Thank you for your loyalty, whether this is your first time reading my work or if you're a longtime supporter.

Be blessed!

Shelia E. Bell
  God's Amazing Girl

More "Perfect Stories About
Imperfect People Like You and Me"

<u>*Teen/Young Adult Titles*</u>
House of Cars
The Life of Payne
The Lollipop Girls
The Righteous Brothers (Coming soon)

<u>*Novels and Novellas*</u>
Cross Road
Forever Ain't Enough
Show A Little Love (*out of print*)
Always Now and Forever Love Hurts
Into Each Life
Sinsatiable
What's Blood Got To Do With It?
Only In My Dreams
The House Husband

<u>*Series Books*</u>
Beautiful Ugly
True Beauty (*sequel to Beautiful Ugly*)

<u>*My Son's Wife Series*</u>
Book 1 - My Son's Wife
Book 2 - My Son's Ex-Wife: The Aftermath
Book 3 - My Son's Next Wife
Book 4 - My Sister My Momma My Wife
Book 5 - My Wife My Baby…And Him
Book 6 - The McCoys of Holy Rock
Book 7 - Dem McCoy Boys
Book 8 - My Brother, My Father…and Me
Book 9 - (Coming Soon)

Real Housewives of Adverse City Series
The Real Housewives of Adverse City 1
The Real Housewives of Adverse City 2
The Real Housewives of Adverse City 3
The Real Housewives of Adverse City 4 (Coming soon)

Anthologies
Bended Knees
Weary to Will
Learning to Love Me

Nonfiction
A Christian's Perspective: Journey Through Grief
How to Life Your Life Like It's Golden
(Even if There's No Pot of Gold at the End of the Rainbow)

If you enjoyed reading "Forever Ain't Enough" or if you have enjoyed reading any books by Shelia E. Bell, please go to your favorite online site and leave a positive review. Reviews help determine the success of an author. It is the ultimate display of support you, as readers, can give.

Whether this is your first time reading a book by me or whether you have followed my literary career from the beginning, I say THANK YOU!

There is no Me without You!

Shelia E. Bell

Contact information
www.sheliaebell.net
www.sheliawritesbooks.com
sheliawritesbooks@yahoo.com
www.facebook.com/sheliawritesbooks
@sheliaebell (Twitter & Instagram)
@literacyrocks (Instagram)

Please join my mailing list for literary updates and new book release information
www.sheliawritesbooks.com